The Class Re

places and incidents are either products of the author's
imagination or are used fictitiously. Any resemblance to actual
people living or dead are entirely coincidental.

Cover Art by Vector Artistry

Danielle,
Welcome to
the reunion!

Previous Novels by Sean McDonough

Beverly Kills
The Terror at Turtleshell Mountain
Rock and Roll Death Trip

For Blair, born at the same time as this book.

And for my friends. Everything warm and decent in this book, I learned alongside all of you.

....Everything in this book that's cold and violent, we'll just say it was there when you found me.

1

Todd stood underneath the streetlight and angled his phone towards his face. The school sign wasn't quite in the frame. He shuffled to the right and lowered the camera just a hair.

Much better. The sign for Saint Regina's was now perfectly positioned in the background over his shoulder. Even better, the snow was starting to fall- big, fat flakes that would look great in the orange light and add some real atmosphere, especially after he fiddled with the contrast and slapped a filter on it.

Todd snapped the selfie. *Perfect.* This would make a great final photo for his article.

I stood there as the snow began to drift from the sky. The old elementary school sign looked exactly like I remembered. The words "Saint Regina Catholic Academy" were the same inlaid gold. The wooden sign was the same vivid red, like Palm Sunday vestments. Everything was exactly the same.

....Everything except me.

Gold. Pure gold. Todd hastily scribbled it down in his Moleskine notebook. Lighting crackled in these hastily scrawled pages. He could feel it. And if this article turned out as good as he thought it might, he might finally have his ticket off of an assistant's desk and onto his own column. All he needed now was a title.

Kerouac 2019.

No, that wouldn't work. He flipped up the collar of his bomber jacket and pulled his wool beanie down tighter on his head. That title was too pretentious. Maybe just, *On the Road in 2019.* Yes, that sounded better. It was a reference without being too excessive.

His phone buzzed in his hand. He flipped it over and saw a text from his mother.

Are you Alive!?!?

He sighed and yanked off a glove so he could text back.

I'm FINE. 5 minutes away.

He never should have told her that he was hitchhiking home. Every five minutes- "Are you okay!?" "Who are you with!?" "Did somebody attack you!?" It was a four hour ride, for Christ's sake. He rode 120 miles with some NYU kids going home for the holidays, and then a Baptist church van from Pittsburgh took him the last 30 miles. They would have dropped him off at his driveway if he'd asked, but Todd had insisted on finishing the last quarter mile on foot, both for the shot by his old school and so that he could take fifteen minutes to decompress before his mother caught him in one of her hour-long death hugs.

He briefly considered taking the long way home, but the icy wind screeching in his ears convinced him otherwise. He got off the sidewalk and cut across the dead, yellow front lawn of the school, heading around back to their pitiful excuse for a "schoolyard." It was a parking lot is what it was; an asphalt parking lot with a pair of basketball hoops and four spray paint "bases" arranged in a poor man's baseball diamond in the corner.

Dumpsters are the right side foul line, he remembered. *Basketball hoop is the left side.*

Shit. Todd was amazed he still remembered all of that. It wasn't as if he ever even played wiffle ball with "the boys" during recess. And yet, he still came to a stop there in left field, right where they always stuck him during gym class. Todd looked towards home plate and was amazed to feel something like...*fondness* warm the cockles of his heart. The teachers had been pious bitches, and the building was a dump, but Saint Regina's Academy had felt like *his* in a way that no school ever had since. Not high school, and certainly not college.

And Todd did have good memories from those years. Not with Chris or the other jerks who pounded on him like he was the tutorial level in a video game, but with his real friends. The same friends he'd be calling as soon as he got home and settled in. He'd met them right here in this school yard, playing *Dragonball Z* and trading Pokemon cards. The other guys had taunted him. They'd call them his "girlfriends," but Todd didn't care. Seventeen years later and they were, without a doubt, the best friends that he'd ever make.

Still swept up in his own wistful nostalgia, Todd turned over his shoulder to look at the old building one more time. So much of it was exactly as he remembered it: the weathered brick facade, the faded black trim around the long windows.

The face looking down at him from one of the windows.

Bullshit. To prove it, Todd stood his ground and fixed his unblinking gaze on the second story window where a blank, featureless face was *not* staring back at him.

It was not a face. It wasn't. It was a smear of falling snow clumped at the corner of the window. A white "head" with darkened indents for "eyes," nothing more. Nobody was hanging around inside the school at 8 o'clock on a Friday night. In fact, nobody was hanging around Saint Regina's at all anymore. Todd could see the heavy padlock around the back doors for himself. The school had gone the way of Sears and Toys R Us.

It was just like those "Virgin Mary reflected on a piece of toast" pictures they used to pass around in religion class. It was all a perception trick; his subconscious mind enforcing a cohesive design that wasn't actually there. The more he looked at the faux-face watching him from the window, the more certain he became that he was right. There was nobody there.

The wind raced over the bare plain of the school yard, icy teeth biting at his ass. *Enough of this crap,* he decided. It was time to get home.

He turned his back on the building once more. As he did, a passage from his single, woebegone attempt at horror fiction rose up within his head:

Humans are the only animal more concerned with being smart than staying alive. If someone puts a fake owl in their garden, the rabbit doesn't venture out to see if its real or not. A dog flees from the sound of thunder and never once stops to wonder if it looks silly.

A human has to know first. In point of fact, the human has to be actively convinced that he needs to be afraid. The human would much rather convince himself that everything is fine so he can get home, embrace his mother, and laugh with his friends until morning light.

Blah blah blah. Seeing his friends sounded good. The rest could stay in his old Intro to Creative Writing class where it belonged.

Todd came to the chain-link fence separating school property from the neighborhood behind it. The fence was still there and, naturally, so was the wide opening cut through the steel links. This was "the neighborhood underground railroad" that he'd referenced in the opening paragraph of his article. Fresh inspiration kindled within Todd as he looked upon that rusty gash once again. He was able to describe it so much more vividly now that he had it in front of him. Todd considered taking out his notebook, but it was just so fucking cold. He'd have to try and remember the prose as best he could.

At some point- maybe one year before I came to the school, or maybe twenty, an enterprising teen had cut a pathway through the steel link fence. With a $15 set of bolt-cutters, that anonymous hero had single handedly cut in half the commute to school for an entire generation. You could finish a 7 AM cartoon and still get to class on time. You could get takeout from Antonio's and bring it back home before it went cold. All it took was someone willing to push back against the walls that held us in.

Todd crouched down. He was a little bigger at twenty-three than he was at eleven.

Nevertheless, the tear in the chainlinks was wide enough that I didn't think I'd have any problems slipping through. Indeed, as soon as I approached the mouth, the portal that will take me back to my childhood home, muscle memory took over. I dipped down at the knees and slid forward in a single motion, easily avoiding the sharp-toothed edges of the sheared steel links. I was halfway through the fence when the heavy hand clamped down on the back of my neck and hauled me backwards with the easy strength of a grown man reeling in an errant puppy.

Todd stopped narrating then, but reality didn't stop. The rough, powerful fingers were still locked tight around his neck. He was still being hauled backwards. Back towards Saint Regina's.

Passing through the fence, Todd had taken great care not to cut himself on the rusty, jagged points of cut metal. The person dragging him back out took the exact opposite care. He deliberately raked Todd along the sharp edges of broken chain link. Todd's throat caught on a jagged tip of sheared metal and his carotid artery tore open in a silent gush.

The hand let him go. Todd dropped, boneless, to the schoolyard asphalt. His blood steamed out in a hot spring around his head. He clamped his hand over the wound, but he may as well have put his thumb over a firehose for all the good that it did. He gurgled blood. His body wanted to twist and spasm on the ground, but a massive boot planted itself on Todd's chest and pinned him in place.

The white-shrouded figure looked down on Todd, watching him die. *His face really does look like snow*, Todd might have thought if he wasn't lost in his dying throes. The killer's face was cloaked in a veil made from lamb's skin of the purest white. The only color to be found lurked in the eye holes. Eyes of rotted brown smoldered deep within the ragged cuts in the shroud- large eyes that might have been called expressive in the face of a kinder person. Blazing from within the hood of Todd's murderer, they could only be called monstrous.

Another seizure ripped through Todd's body. He felt very cold, even though the heat rose around him in a haze of steam. Strangely, he felt no fear. There had been no time for fear. One moment he'd been taking a shortcut home. The next, he was nothing. He was numb limbs and gushing blood. He was fading. He was emptying.

The Damned Fra Anjelico watched Todd's death convulsions, soaking in every detail, missing nothing. The boy was bathed in color, even as his eyes turned bland and his life dulled. The palette of his death... it was magnificent.

When he was certain that Todd was dead, the Fra grabbed his ankle and dragged the body away from the fence. A thick trail of blood lingered behind the corpse, but the Fra was not concerned. The snow was already sticking to the ground, and more was falling thicker and faster around the Damned Fra and his prize. The forecast called for upwards of 48 inches by midnight. The blood would be concealed within the hour.

It reminded the Damned Fra of a Buddhist monk's sand mandala- an exquisite work of art drawn in sand and then wiped away, living on only in the memory of those who witnessed it.

Dragging Todd's body back towards the school, the Damned Fra reflected that it was a fitting way to begin his own work.

2

The snow in Pine Hollow, Pennsylvania was already an inch deep when Vickie Fields got off the Amtrak train. The cold clamped down around her like a vice and the wind blew slow and frigid past her ears. *"My, my. Vickie Fields."* the creeping breeze whispered. *"We haven't seen you in forever. It's good to have you back. I hope it's not too cold for you, but I'm sure you remember how we like it here in Pine Hollow- the sun doesn't shine, every pipe is frozen, and every walkway is an ice rink. World without warmth, Amen."*

Vickie expected nothing less. She hadn't even bothered to glance at the forecast before she hopped on the train in sunny Charleston, she just dug out her winter jacket and snow boots and braced herself for the worst.

She stepped out from the warm confines of the train station. Much like her best friend Todd had done only minutes earlier, Vickie turned up the collar on her peacoat and pulled her hat down more firmly over her earbuds. She set out down Hooverton street, away from the station. The stores she passed on the street flashed by like tracks from a greatest hits album. She walked past the 7-Eleven where they used to loiter in the parking lot. Earth 3 Comics was still in business, even if the store was currently dark and buttoned up ahead of the storm. Ah, and here was the Salvation Army store: Western Pennsylvania's premier destination for only the finest 90s band tees and men's cargo pants. Vickie had a flashback to a Korn t-shirt that she'd sworn was the height of cool back in sophomore year and felt a kind of disgusted pride in herself.

She walked by Saint Regina's Academy without stopping. The school was dark now, and not because of Christmas break. She'd heard about the school closure on Facebook, a victim of low enrollments and budget cuts. Vickie had felt no nostalgia then and she felt even less now.

Vickie's house was on the opposite end of the neighborhood. She didn't need to take the shortcut through the schoolyard. She only had to do the same thing she always did when she passed by Saint Regina's. She kept her head down and put the building behind her as quickly as possible.

Snow sucked. It made the whole world hostile to the touch. It made even the simplest tasks a thousand times harder. It was still one of her favorite things about Charleston- the knowledge that she could wake up on a January day and be absolutely certain that there were no snow-clogged walkways to shovel and no chilly slush to soak into her socks.

Still, there was a small window of time where there was no denying the beauty of the falling snow. For Vickie Fields, that window opened as she hung a left at the Cold Spell diner and entered the side streets where her childhood home awaited. The snow had fallen over the neighborhood in a perfect, undisturbed sheet. Vickie could look out over empty streets of white, with nary a footprint to prove that anyone else existed in the entire world. Alone in the silence beneath the drifting flakes and the orange glow of the streetlights, she was the owner of her own pocket universe.

Tomorrow she would hate it. She would hate being recruited to dig out the cars. She would hate the dirty gray snow hugging every surface. She would hate it all until she could get back to her apartment where the winter temperatures were rarely lower than 50. But for the five minutes it would take her to get home, she allowed herself to be taken in by the beauty of the snowy night.

Vickie climbed the short flight of porch steps and finally reached the front door of the small ranch house she'd grown up in. The old house key still hung on her "Alohomora" keychain, right next to her apartment key, and it slipped into the lock as easily as it always did.

Of course it still does. She felt a twinge of guilt every time she thought that way. As if her parents would ever change the locks on her. Or disown her. Or call her-

"Vick!"

Her dad was out of his recliner the moment she came through the door. He was using the cane, which she didn't like, but he moved quickly and when he pulled her into a hug she felt the comforting, familiar strength of his beefy arms.

"Oh, kid," he said into her ear. His unshaven face rasped against her cheek. "Oh, kid. Welcome home."

She hugged him back hard. "Happy to be back," she said. She tried to guide him back to the chair. "Come on, sit down."

He shrugged her off. "I'm just stiff because it's cold. I saw Doctor O'Brien last week; she said I'm healthy as could be."

Vickie hoped so. Her father had been a pipefitter before a fall off a ladder left him with a shattered leg and two cracked vertebrae. He'd recovered well enough, but she always worried whenever the cane came out.

"That just means you need to sit *and* you need a blanket," Vickie pressed. She crossed the living room in swift, purposeful steps, moving as confidently as if she'd lived here only days ago, instead of years. For all intents and purposes, she may as well have. The same brass lamps still cast the room in yellow light. The TV was a little sharper, but it sat on the same wooden stand. She flipped the top off the storage ottoman by the couch and was confronted by the exact collection of afghan blankets she expected to find. She rooted around until she found her dad's favorite, the one knitted out of intertwined black and gold yarn, and brought it back over to the chair.

"Alright," he said, settling down into the plaid-patterned recliner. "I'll sit. I'll sit." He took the blanket from her and made a grand show of tucking it around his legs. "How was the train?" he asked.

"Not bad. A whole bench in the observation car to myself and the whole Timmverse on Amazon Prime. Where's mom? Work?"

"She was able to swing an overnight shift so she can be home through Christmas. She has a *very* full week lined up for the two of you."

Vickie pulled her cheeks back in a grin/grimace. She flashed her dad two very exaggerated thumbs up, leaving him laughing as she went to the fridge. She opened the door, hoping against hope... Yes, *Antonio's*! She took the pizza box out of the fridge and put two slices into the toaster oven. The third, she brought back into the living room and bit into it cold.

"Mmm," Vickie said. She closed her eyes, savoring the flavor.

"You've got sauce on your face," her dad said.

Vickie thumbed at the corner of her mouth.

"No. Other side. There, you got it."

He continued to stare at her anyway. He only hastily turned his gaze back towards the TV once he saw the knowing smirk decorating his daughter's face.

Vickie leaned against the door frame and shook her head fondly. She knew exactly what he was thinking about as he looked at her face. She saw the exact same thing in reverse as she took in her father's features.

His hair was long gone, but it had once been thick and black like hers was now. And she had his thin nose and hazel eyes. And she had his appetite and the sturdy figure that went with it. She was tall like he was. And she had his corny sense of humor.

But her dad couldn't so much as draw a stick figure. And he didn't know anything about the Timmverse. Or Harry Potter. And he was perfectly content to spend the rest of his days in the small town that he'd never left.

But that didn't stop him from driving a U-haul through the night to set his only daughter up in a new city seven hundred miles away. He'd hugged her tight then too, after she was moved in and after they'd eaten the dinner that he begrudgingly allowed her to pay for. "I want to tell you to call me if you have any problems," he'd said. "But, if I'm being honest, I'm not sure how much wisdom I'm going to have for anything you're life's going to throw at you." He opened the door to the U-haul and looked back at her one last time. "Good thing then that I'm sure you know better than I do anyway."

He'd smiled at her before driving away. The same way he was smiling at her now as he met her eye. Vickie swallowed her chunk of pizza and loosed a full-throated belch. She knew exactly what reaction she would get, and she was rewarded with the pure, simple love flooding her father's features.

"I'm fine by the way," he called out. "I wasn't saving that for myself or anything!"

"You are fine," Vickie said. "Don't think Mom didn't tell me about the diet the doctor put you on."

He waved her away. "Your mother's trying to starve me for the life insurance money. I want one of those slices."

She shook her head.

"Give me a piece or I'm going to ask about your love life."

Vickie blanched. "Way to kill my appetite," she said. She went into the kitchen and came back with one of the pieces from the toaster.

Her father took a big bite from the proffered slice and sank deeper into the chair. He closed his eyes, lost in bliss. "It always tastes better after you give the cheese a little time to thicken up."

He cracked one eye open. "So. Dating anyone?"

Vickie picked up the remote and pointed it at him. "Mute," she said. "I'm muting you."

"I'm not going to pry," her dad said. "I just want to make sure you know that if you want to bring, you know-" there was the slightest hesitation, "A girl home, you can."

"I know," Vickie said. "You told me. You hugged me. The cake was appreciated. But I just want you to know, it is possible for you to love and support me and still never ask me anything about my personal life. Ever."

He held out his hand. "Deal."

She ignored his hand and kissed him on the head. "It's nice to be home, Dad."

Somebody knocked at their front door then.

And again.

And again.

The pounding on the door became a machine gun staccato. Vickie's dad rolled his eyes. "You two have magnets in your asses. Whenever one of you gets close, the other one just gets yanked right on over."

"I texted her I was home," Vickie said. But she was already beelining towards the door, swinging it open and eagerly meeting a whirlwind of red hair and flying scarves.

"Vickie!"

Bridget careened into her, smashing both of them against the coat closet as she wrapped Vickie in a hug that would put a python to shame. Vickie gave as good as she got. She wrenched Bridget up in a half-assed twirl that ended with both of them crumpled in the doorway, melted snow soaking through their pants, laughing their asses off.

"Stop," Bridget protested, gasping for air. "I lost my glasses."

"Here," Vickie said, picking her friend's glasses out from a puddle of melting snow. She dried them on the bottom of her shirt, noting with some surprise how thin and transparent the frames were. It was a far cry from the thick, round "Clark Kent" glasses Bridget had worn since middle school.

And her hair looks darker. I think she dyed it.

"Welcome home!" Bridget shouted.

"Thank yah," Vickie drawled in a terrible Elvis impression. "Thank yah vereh much." Her voice returned to normal. "Did Todd get in yet?"

Bridget shrugged. "I texted him but I haven't heard anything back. Did he tell you? He's *hitchhiking* home!"

Vickie laughed. "He told me. He's such a fucking trope."

But she said it fondly. Todd was *their* fucking trope. Vickie and Bridget had been best friends since nursery school, but they'd adopted Todd in kindergarten and never let him go. They were Team Rocket. Buffy, Willow, and Xander. The Defenders, minus that jackass Iron Fist. It was great seeing Bridge, but the gang wouldn't be truly back together until Todd was on the couch with them, ranting about the debt *Sharknado* owed to *Sharktopus*.

Bridget looked over Vickie's shoulder and waved. "Hey, Mr. F! Mrs. F at the hospital?"

"Yeah, Bridge," he said. "Minding the shop all by myself tonight. Also, yes. You and Vickie can go out."

"What?"

"That's the next question one of you is about to ask. 'Can Vickie go out even though she's only been home five minutes and her father loves her and misses her?' And it's fine. But the snow's going to get a lot worse. I want you to sleep over at Bridget's or Todd's or wherever you guys wind up. No driving after there's more than three inches on the ground."

"You just want to watch the 76ers by yourself in peace," Vickie said.

"That's not true, Vickie. I would love for you to stay home so you can tell me all about your job, and your friends, and your girlfriend, and-"

"I'm gone!" Vickie shouted. She grabbed Bridget by the wrist and pulled her out the door. "Leaving! Farewell! Adieu!" She slammed the door behind her with a definitive force that she didn't truly feel.

-    -   -

"I love your dad," Bridget said as they crunched through the snow.

"Makes me think he deserves a better Christmas present," Vickie remarked. "But then I'd have to get my mom a better present, and then what does that leave for my Xbox budget?"

"Well, last Christmas you told them you were gay, so I'm sure they'll appreciate anything that isn't another bombshell."

"You mean it's a bad time to tell them about the tattoo of the Thirteenth Doctor on my ass?"

"At least tell them about the other twelve first," Bridget cracked, and then they were both howling, holding onto each other for support as they made their way down the walk. "Oh, it's been too long!" Vickie cried, emphasizing her point with a good shake.

Bridget squeezed her again. "Well, don't worry about it too much. I assure you, absolutely nothing has changed."

Vickie drew back in mock surprise. "In Pine Hollow? *You're kidding!*"

They came to Bridget's Ford Escape, and Vickie stopped in her tracks. "Oh, shit," she exclaimed. "That's not the same."

Bridget winced, even though the damage was no surprise to her. The grill on her 2002 SUV was punched in, and the hood was held down with a ratchet strap. "The deer send their love…. just not that one."

"You hit a deer!? Why didn't you tell me?"

Bridget shrugged. "Happened a few weeks ago. Tips between Christmas and New Years'll be good. I'll get it covered."

"You're not going to be working New Year's Eve, are you?"

Bridget looked away. She kicked a clump of snow.

"Bridget!" Vickie cried, scandalized. New Year's Eve was their annual Carrie Fisher marathon. Todd had finally gotten them to cave and add *Sorority Row* to the lineup this year.

"My boss is making me," Bridget lied. "I couldn't get out of it." In truth, she was hoping to go back to school for a dental hygienist certificate, and the numbers were already daunting enough without coughing up $700 for auto repairs. She knew Vickie wouldn't judge her for it, but in a lot of ways, her understanding would be worse. The town was divided into two halves- prosperous and scraping by. Vickie had landed on the good side by a hair split in half thanks to a generous settlement after her dad's accident, but that half a hair covered more incidentals than Vickie realized.

Vickie shook her head but, thankfully didn't pry. Her distress had blown away like a storm out to sea. "We'll do it the next night," she said. "Or the night after. And you can get me and Todd a table at your restaurant on New Year's."

Bridget laughed. "So long as you don't mind eating next to the kitchen. At 5:30. With a $75 a plate minimum."

Vickie batted her eyelashes. "I'm sure money is no option for my handsome escort," she said. "Oh, and do make sure the bill's given directly to him, please."

Bridge's phone buzzed. "Ah, speak of the devil."

"Todd?"

"Yeah." She checked the text. "He says he's not coming home until tomorrow."

Vickie snorted. "You know that he's freezing his ass off on the side of the road somewhere and he's just too proud to admit it."

3

They decided to get a late dinner at the Cold Spell. The diner was still bustling, even as the snow outside began to fall faster, but they managed to grab one of the last open booths. Bridget looked at a menu. "Alright, I'm gonna get the tenders. And you're going to have…" Bridge touched her forehead and squinted her eyes shut. "Don't tell me." She waved her free hand through the air. "You're ordering… the Monte Cristo!"

"I'm just gonna get a grilled chicken sandwich," Vickie said.

Bridget gasped. She clutched her chest, scandalized.

"I ate a slice of Antonio's before you got here!" Vickie said.

Bridget's eyes narrowed. "This is that Jenny's doing, isn't it? You're going to have to break up with her."

"We're not even dating," Vickie said. "She's just… cool. And I need at least one friend who's courteous enough to share fitness pointers with me."

"What do you mean?" Bridget asked.

"I mean I can see your muscles through your sweater, Supergirl. How many times a week do you go to the gym?"

Bridget flushed. She folded her arms on the table, which only called more attention to her toned biceps. It wasn't that she'd lost weight, Bridge had always been tiny, but Vickie had felt it when they hugged. There was a firmness to Bridget's physique that had never been there before.

The waitress arrived. Vickie caved and ordered the Monte Cristo (she blamed Bridge for putting the idea in her head). The food arrived fast and went fast, as it always did, but the conversation continued long after their plates were clean. The two of them texted each other every day, but there was no substitute for the real thing. The blow by blow of Vickie's first year fully out of the closet. ("Educational," Vickie said with a wink.) Bridget's adventures with the motley crew she worked with at the restaurant. ("If Kathy tries to set me up with her son, 'the gamer,' one more time…" Bridge swore to Vickie's howls of laughter.) They both loved Todd, but privately they were happy to have some time with just the two of them.

"How's your job?" Bridget asked. "What are you working on?"

Vickie took her phone out and pulled up a photo folder with some of her works in progress. She slid it across the table for Bridget's inspection.

"This one is a commission I'm doing for someone online. Charcoal and pastels."

"Ugh," Bridge said, zooming in closer so she could see more detail. Vickie had all the characters from *My Hero Academia* sketched out around a billiards table. She'd only just started the coloring, but Bridget could tell the finished product was going to be fantastic. "I still can't believe you get paid for this," Bridget said. "I hate you."

"Well, it's not all that glamorous. Next week I need to start on a commission of Sonic the Hedgehog's feet."

"...But Sonic always wears shoes."

"Oh, Bridget. How I wish that were true," Vickie said.

Bridget shuddered and swiped left to the next picture. "What's this one?"

Vickie made a face. "That's something for my day job. Just a coupon flyer for an organic grocery store. Glorified copy and paste."

Bridget brought up the next picture. It was a hand drawn sketch of a storefront with an awning lined with red lights and a facade of old wooden planks. Vickie had given it a gritty style with short, sketchy lines in colored pencil.

"Is this the store?" she asked.

"Oh, no. That's actually cool. It's a promo poster we're doing for the Pour House- that bar I'm always telling you about. The bands there are out of this fucking world."

"It sounds great," Bridge said.

"You should come see it," Vickie said. "You should see the harbor festival. You should see the Terrace Theatre. You should see my new apartment. Bridge, you really ought to just move to South Carolina."

Bridget looked up from the last dab of ketchup she was trying to coax from the glass bottle.

"I mean it," Vickie said. "You could get a waitress job down there in five seconds. You'd love my friend Bobbi with an i. The three of us could get an apartment together for next to nothing. And my friend Bobby with a y… well, I think you'd *really* like him."

Bridget suddenly didn't know what to do with her hands. She focused on a rip in the vinyl directly over Vickie's left shoulder. "I'm set up here," she murmured.

"Bridget. It's Pine fucking Hollow. Nice to come back to for Christmas, sucks to stick around for February. Every year you're exposed to this place makes you twenty percent more likely to develop a Steelers tramp stamp and a crush on your cousin. There's a better way to live, Bridge. I mean- do you know how amazing it is to just not feel *crazy* every day?"

"I-"

"No," Vickie cut her off. "You don't. Because you're still living here where everyone thinks you're a freak. I'm not going to tell you I'm Queen of the Harbor, but I actually *LIKE* where I live. There's a bar that shows *The Walking Dead* on Sunday night instead of football. And the coffee shop across the street from my place? They don't just have books on all the tables, you've got to get there early on Saturdays or all the Neil Gaiman books are gone."

"It sounds great, Vickie."

"It *is* great," Vickie emphasized. "And I want you to experience it with me. Will you at least think about it?"

Bridget's phone buzzed as a text came in. She slipped it out of her jacket, grateful for a chance to look away from Vickie's expectant gaze. She started to type out a response.

"Is that Todd?" Vickie asked.

"Huh?" Bridget said.

"You keep texting somebody," Vickie prompted. "Is it Todd moving his fingers to keep warm?"

Bridge laughed, but it came out awkward and out of rhythm, like a hand carelessly splayed across piano keys. "Just my mom," she said. "She says hi." Bridget quickly stuffed the phone away. Out of sight, out of mind.

"If you're flirting with him, you can just tell me. I'm fine being the Harry to your Ron and Hermione. I'd like it better if one of you had a hot, gay sister, but-"

"It's not Todd, Vickie!" Bridget said.

"But you *are* flirting?!" Vickie accused. "Who is he? What's his name? Where'd you meet him?" She leaned forward, willing to physically pull the information out of Bridge if she had to.

Bridget bit her lip and tucked her chin. She self-consciously swirled her last chicken tender in the honey mustard. At first Vickie thought she was just being awkward, but then it hit her.... Bridge was trying not to smile.

"Bridget! Tell me!"

Bridget squirmed in the booth. A nervous giggle almost seeped out of her, but she bit down on her knuckle to keep it in.

"Bridget. Teresa. Fallon," Vickie warned.

"You're going to judge me..." Bridget said.

"You look happy, that's all I care about," Vickie assured her. "Come on, tell me."

"You promise you won't judge me?"

"Oh, for God's sake, yes! Now out with it!"

His name rose up suddenly then. Perhaps that was best. Bridget had been thinking of a way to tell Vickie for weeks now, but she hadn't been able to think of a way to say it without sounding defensive. This was the answer. To simply say his name because she could no longer bear to keep it to herself for one more second.

"Chris Castellano!" she blurted out.

Vickie's jaw dropped. Her eyes swelled like balloons. Bridget giggled. She knew that Vickie would be shocked.

....But then she looked like she might be having a stroke.

"Vickie?"

Vickie sat back. The shock passed, but her features were a swirling combination of confusion and suspicion.

"I know it's weird," Bridge plowed on. "But the gym where he works is right next to the restaurant, and sometimes we'd see each other coming and going. And then one night he came into the restaurant, and another night I tried a trial membership at the gym and we just kind of..." She left it out there for Vickie to pick up.

Vickie did not pick it up. Vickie continued to silently evaluate Bridget the way you'd look at someone who might be coming down with the flu. *Or the plague.*

"I know. It's weird," Bridge repeated.

Vickie found her voice. "Yeah. It's… unexpected."

"It just sort of happened. Neither of us really had anyone to hang out with. You and Todd are away, all of his friends went out of state too."

"You mean he didn't get into Yale?"

Bridget frowned. "He's nice, Vickie."

"He wasn't nice in high school," Vickie said. "He was an asshole. He was actually the leader of a whole merry band of assholes."

Bridget tried to shrug, like she didn't have all the same memories that Vickie did. Bridget with her new glasses and her new dyed hair. "We're not in high school anymore," she said.

"How long has this been going on?" Vickie pressed.

"Just a month. I didn't say anything because we haven't said anything. I mean, we've, you know, talked. But not *that* talk. Not yet. But…"

That barely restrained smile again. It practically beamed out of her.

"He's special."

Special ed, Vickie thought, but held back at the last moment. She took a deep breath. *Be supportive. Be supportive. Minds are like parachutes, et cetera, et cetera.*

"He does have kind of a young Vin Diesel thing going on," Vickie allowed.

"He does, doesn't he?" Bridget gushed. "He just texted me, some of his friends are home for christmas too and he wants us to meet up! Please say you'll come. *Please*!?"

VIckie blanched. "His friends? What could we possibly do with his friends?"

"Just hang out. Talk. Drink. They're cool."

"Are you forgetting I know these people? Who's there? Pete Arrogate? Ellen Cutter? Why don't I just call myself a fat freak and save the gas money?"

"Come on, Vickie," Bridget said. "Don't let a stupid high school grudge-"

"They treated us like shit!" Vickie yelled. "Maybe you forgot, but I didn't!"

Bridget didn't say anything else, but she didn't have to. Bridge had lived through it too. In elementary gym class they never played on the same team because they were always the last two kids picked. In middle school they were punching bags for girls whose breasts came in first. In high school their reputation had been cemented- weirdos. Freaks. Sluts or prudes, depending on the purpose of the moment.

And Vickie had a memory of her own. One she'd never shared with Bridget. She'd tutored Chris during junior year. Handsome, muscular, varsity wrestling captain Chris Castellano. She was looking to put another extracurricular on her college applications. He was looking to pass chemistry.

Except, what the handsome, muscular, varsity wrestling captain had been really looking for was someone to do his final project for him. And, if Vickie played along, Chris had mentioned parties. He'd talked about bringing her along places and putting in a good word with the football team and the lacrosse team on her behalf. He favored her with a smile he usually reserved for cheerleaders. "What do you say, Fields? Think you can help me out?"

Vickie couldn't look him in the eye. Not back then. Blushing bright red, she focused on a bookshelf just beyond his shoulder.

"I'll help you, Chris. But you've got to do your own work. I can't-"

"Nobody fucking likes you, Fields. I'm giving you a chance here, and all you have to do is just copy and paste what you're already doing. Come on, don't be a bitch about this."

He spoke low, it was the library after all, but Vickie heard him loud and clear. Maybe she heard him somewhere that had decided that fourteen years of abuse was more than enough. All Vickie knew was that she calmly sat up straight in her chair and looked him dead in the eye.

"Okay, Chris. I guess it makes sense when you put it that way. Let's get started by looking for some references."

Sitting at the library computer, Vickie pulled up Google. While Chris watched, she typed a question into the search bar.

Which 'roid-head, Hulk Hogan wannabe is going to be working at McDonalds after graduation? And does he have a gummy worm for a penis?

Vickie swiveled away from the monitor and leaned back in her seat. "Oh, look," she said. "One result."

Chris had stormed out of the library without so much as a word, and Vickie's only regret was the extra abuse that Bridget had to deal with for the next few weeks.

"Call animal control! We got dogs on the loose!"

"What reeks? I'll bet Red forgot to change her tampon again"

"Yo, Vick. What're you going to the girl's bathroom for? Finally get your birth certificate changed?"

Bridget picked up her phone.

"What are you doing?" Vickie asked.

"I'm telling Chris I'll see him later."

"Bridge-"

"I can hardly show you a bad time on your first night back, can I?"

"I can tag along. It won't be the worst thing in the world."

"Forget it. I've got Bobbi-i and Bobby-y to compete with, and I'm sure they don't drag you to parties you don't want to go to."

Vickie leaned across the table snatched the phone away from her before Bridge could hit send.

"Vickie-"

Vickie pulled back out of Bridget's reach. She backspaced away Bridge's response and hastily tapped away at her own reply. "Do you call him sweet cheeks? Well, you do now."

"Vickie, don't!"

Vickie kept typing, safely out of Bridge's reach. "On... my...way... sweet cheeks." She hit send. Waited. "Aw, 'Can't wait.' And he added a kissy face. That actually is kinda nice."

She handed the phone back. Bridget took it with some reverence.

"We'll have fun," Bridget promised.

"Well, you'll have fun. I'll be drunk and that's close enough," Vickie said.

"I just have to stop at my house and then we'll go," Bridget said.

"What do we need to stop at your house for?"

Bridget signaled for the check.

"Bridget," Vickie pressed. "What are we stopping at your house for?"

"...I want to put on a different bra," she muttered.

Vickie pressed her hands tightly together. She scrunched her eyes tight and bowed her head as if in prayer. "Are you and your handsome, popular boyfriend going to give me the *Stranger Things* treatment, Bridge?" she asked.

"What?"

"I mean, are we going to this party just so you can get laid while I sit outside like a miserable third wheel and get devoured by the first interdimensional monstrosity that passes by?"

"Oh, God. Of course not."

"Don't you Barb me, Fallon" Vickie warned. "I swear to God."

"Nobody is getting Barb-ed!" Bridget insisted.

"Does Chris have a pool?"

"We're not even going to Chris' house."

"Don't avoid the question," Vickie said. "I don't care where we're going. Is there a pool or not?"

Bridget winced. "Well... The good news is there's no pool."

4

Chris let out a breath he didn't even know he was holding.
On my way, sweet cheeks.

...Weird choice of words, but Bridge was weird. He'd learned that early on. And it hadn't taken long for him to learn that he liked it.

Okay. Can't wait.

She was coming. That was what mattered.

"Yo, Chris! You playing or what?"

"Yeah, hang on." He jogged back over to his place next to Pete at the beer pong table. Alex and Ellen were already waiting on the opposite end of the table.

"Every year we take all of our best clients to the Tulane-LSU game for a big tailgate party" Pete continued. "This year, I talked to one of my frat brothers who's an engineer. He came out and we put this huge-ass platform in the back of a pickup truck so we could rip two-story beer bongs."

Alex laughed. "That's how you close a fucking sale!"

"It was insane. You guys should come out to NOLA for March Madness. I can get us a crazy discount on floor seats."

"For sure," Alex said. "I checked the flights and it's only four-fifty if I fly into LaFayette. I can definitely make that happen."

"Sweet, come in Friday night and I'll pick you up after work. Ellen, you game? I'll sweeten the deal with the best ribs you ever had."

Ellen snorted. "Please don't tell me that I need to leave Texas to get good barbecue, Pete. Give me a date and I'll think about it, but I'm clerking part time at a law firm in the spring. If there's a big trial going on, then I'm out."

Pete grinned and shook his head. "Alright, alright. I can work with that, just don't sue me for lost wages. What about you, Chris? Don't leave me hanging."

If I can scrape up four hundred dollars for a plane ticket, Chris thought. *And a hundred for a game ticket. And another two hundred to cover beer and food for the weekend.*

But what he said was, "I'll try. I'm signed for a fight in February. If I get the win, there's a five hundred dollar bonus up for grabs."

"Then that ticket's already as good as bought!" That's what someone would have said last year. Last year, his friends had all gone crazy when he'd earned a spot on the roster with a regional MMA promotion called "Steel City Strikers." Eight months ago, Alex and Pete had actually flown in for his first fight. They were in the front row when Chris got knocked out by a flying knee in the first round. Four months later, they were all watching the live stream when he dropped a unanimous decision loss in his second fight.

Tonight, nobody said a word. Pete smiled awkwardly and offered a half shrug. Alex made a performance of ensuring that the cups on the table were perfectly aligned.

In the dim light, Chris felt his face glow hot. "Hand me a side beer?" he asked hastily.

Ellen handed him a Bud Light. Chris cracked open the beer and took a swig. "Listen, I texted Bridget Fallon. She's gonna come hang with us."

Across the table, Alex stopped mid-shot with his arm cocked back at the elbow. "Bridget who?"

Ellen, who never forgot a face, cut in. "The redhead who did stage crew. Looks a little like Chucky from *Rugrats*." Chris' expression didn't change, but the beer can crumpled as his hand tightened involuntarily.

"Oh, yeah. Red." Alex shot and missed the table completely. Chris' free hand dropped reflexively and snagged the ball out of mid-air. He tossed it back across the table. A little harder than he needed to.

"You guys'll like her. She's cool. Vickie Fields is gonna come too."

"Whoa!" a voice shouted from down the hall. Tommy came bursting through the double doors, still buckling his belt. "Hold on, what's that about girls?" he asked. He cast his eyes wildly from side to side, as if there were girls hiding in the shadows behind the columns.

"Chris pulled two blasts from the past," Pete said. "Either one single?"

"Bridget's not," he said quickly. "Vickie's-"

Ellen snorted. "None of you are Vickie Field's type," she said.

Tommy threw his arms wide, putting himself on display. "She doesn't like nice guys who know how to make a girl laugh?" he asked.

"She doesn't like dicks."

"Cut me a break, Ellen. I didn't know your brother was in rehab when I made that hillbilly heroin joke."

"He means she's a lesbian, idiot," Alex said. He hesitated and pivoted towards Ellen. "That is what you meant, right?"

Ellen sighed. "Yes. That's what I meant." As Class President, Ellen followed their entire grade on social media- it would make facilitating the class reunion that much easier. As such, she was well aware of Vickie "The Future is Female" Fields and her preferences- both political and sexual.

"That's fine by me. We could use some entertainment," Pete said.

"Be cool," Chris warned.

"I am cool," Pete said. "Go ahead, invite the lesbos."

"Bridget's not gay," Chris snapped.

"Take it easy. She's not your sister."

"Just don't be an asshole."

Pete laughed. He had the kind of booming chuckle that could take a few degrees off the temperature of any conversation. That laugh undoubtedly had something to do with his status as the youngest ad sales manager at the Superdome. "I'm just fucking around," he said. "We had a gay brother in the frat. Good dude. Killer keg stands. I still meet him for lunch sometimes."

Pete broke off as Ellen tried to bounce a shot off the table. He swatted for it but the ping pong ball sailed over his hand and into the center cup.

"Shit!" Pete said. He handed a drink to Chris and drained his own cup.

Chris drank quickly as well. He set the cup down and casually turned back to his phone.

Let me know when you're here. I really can't wait.

He sensed movement to his side and stuffed the phone away before anyone could see. Tommy squeezed his shoulder. "You said you got another fight coming up?" he asked.

Chris shrugged. "Yeah, this guy's big, but he's only had a few fights too. I already watched a little tape and he can be sloppy when he's striking. If I can make him eat some good counters, I really think I...." Chris trailed off, but Tommy slapped him hard on the back regardless. "You're gonna fucking kill him, man. Just let me know when tickets go on sale and I'm in." He put another beer in front of Chris and winked. "Just don't start cutting weight yet."

Chris laughed. "Not tonight... Thanks, Tommy."

"Oh shit," Tommy murmured, fixated on the sight of Ellen stretching with her arms held high above her head. "My Christ, the body on that fucking woman."

Pete snickered. "Fifty-eighth time's the charm, right, Tommy?"

"That's called persistence, my man. Just you wait. I'm gonna have her sucking my cock in Mrs. Simmon's room. Same room where I first saw her back in third grade."

Ellen noticed Tommy looking. She put her arms down and stepped slightly behind Alex, using him as a shield against Tommy's leering gaze.

Chris and Pete both laughed. Pete slugged Tommy in the shoulder. "There's always the fifty-ninth time," he said.

Across the table, Alex took a sip from his side beer and abruptly started sputtering. Suds ran down his chin and onto the front of his shirt. Eyes bulging, he looked into his cup and finally cleared the block his throat. "Yo, what the fuck?!"

Guffawing, Pete slammed the table, eyes scrunched tight against tears of laughter.

Alex's eyes narrowed. "What the fuck did you do?"

Still laughing, Pete reached into his pocket and produced a plastic milk bottle. He shook the empty bottle and rolled it across the table towards Alex. "I left that milk by the radiator all day, just for you, buddy."

Chris and Tommy laughed along with him. Ellen rolled her eyes, but a small smile tugged at the corner of her mouth nonetheless. Revulsion and laughter went to war on Alex's face. He flung the bottle back at Pete, who batted it aside playfully. "Oh, it's gonna be like that tonight?" Alex challenged. "Alright, game on, Peterbilt. Motherfucker."

"Hey," Ellen said. "Speaking of games. Can we play please?"

"You want to go first?" Pete asked Chris.

The phone buzzed again in Chris' pocket. He didn't take it out, not with everybody looking at him, but the smile on his face stretched a little wider. In that moment, everything in his life was exactly how he wanted it to be. "Sure, give me the rock," he said.

Pete handed him the ping pong ball. Chris snagged it and shot, barely bothering to aim. He knew what was going to happen next. He felt it tingling in his fingers before the ball even left his hand.

And Chris wasn't disappointed. His shot dropped into the center cup with a hearty *plunk*.

5

She is so going to owe me for this.

That was the tune Vickie had been singing in her head for the last fifteen minutes as they drove through the snow. The song began, *Brid-GET is going to owe me for this. Yeah, Brid-GET is going to owe me for this,* and then it just kind of continued like that in a loop.

The problem was, Vickie kept trying to think of terrible, boring, miserable activities to put Bridget through as revenge, but she kept getting stuck trying to imagine something that her stupid, terrible, amazing best friend wouldn't sit through to make Vickie happy.

This would be a lot easier if she weren't so goddamn wonderful, Vickie groused.

Vickie had genuinely meant to be magnanimous. Bridget was her best friend. Vickie wanted to support her, even if that meant gritting her teeth and enduring a few hours with a bunch of jackasses who should have stayed in her high school yearbook where they belonged.

But that was before Bridget had told her where they were going. Vickie had figured they were all at a bar. Or maybe somebody's house. Vickie could have handled that.

But… *this.* How the hell had she actually agreed to *this?*

They swung into the parking lot. The shadow of the building rose up to fill the windshield before them. Bridget glanced over at her and Vickie smiled back, feeling like she had to stick fish hooks in her cheeks to do the job.

"You said you didn't care where we were going," Bridget reminded her.

Vickie exhaled hard through her nose. "Yeah? Well, now I care."

"At least there's no pool!" Bridget said. Big grin. Wide eyes. Like a puppy wagging its tail after it peed on the rug. A puppy that knew it should be in trouble.

Vickie wished there was a pool. And a Demogorgon. Anything would be better than the sight of the old building looming behind a ripped flour sack of powdery snow. Two stories of brick wall. Tall windows with black trim, like the openings in a wasp's nest. If she were going to paint it, the only medium that could do it justice would be thick, dark ink set against a backdrop of pure black.

Saint Regina Catholic Academy.

"How about we build an igloo in the parking lot instead?" Vickie asked. "We can appropriate some Inuit culture and build a giant igloo. And get frostbite, lose some toes, and in the morning I'll *still* say, 'It could have been worse. Better to never wear flip flops again than to step foot in Saint Regina Academy one more time."

"Don't think of it as going back to Saint Regina's. Think of it like… dancing on the school's grave!" Bridget said.

"If we have to climb through a window, you're boosting me in first."

"We don't have to climb through a window. Alex-"

"Fucking Alex is here!?'

"Alex's dad is the realtor trying to sell the school," Bridge said, talking over Vickie's outburst. "His parents are away for the weekend and he took the key. We've got the whole place to ourselves. No neighbors, no cops- It's perfect."

"Perfect if I decide to finally kill one of them," Vickie grumbled.

Bridge brought the car around to the back of the school, in line with a black Jeep Cherokee. Alex's Jeep was right where Chris said it would be- behind the dumpsters, underneath the old sycamore tree. Where it had at least some protection from the snow.

"And how do we get back out?" Vickie questioned.

"Chris says that Pete-" Bridget paused, waiting for another outburst from Vickie. None came, but the brunette's scowl said enough. "Pete's brother plows driveways. They're giving him fifty bucks to come by tomorrow morning and clear a path out for us."

They got out of the SUV with snow already almost to their knees. The girls were only wearing jeans, and the damp cold gnawed through the denim, hungry for the skin underneath. Icy wind ripped at their scarves and hats and they tucked their faces down against it.

Still, Vickie spared a moment to stare up at the old building once again. The same old brick and old ideas.

But it's empty now, she reminded herself. What she really saw was just the husk. The school was closed. The nuns were gone. The religion classes were gone.

All that's left are the bullies.

Vickie stood there as the snow piled up around her. The wind howled again, pushing her towards the school.

"Oh, my God, it's so cold!" Bridge yelled. She broke into a run.

Vickie cast her head down and broke into a shuffling run after her. *Just like old times,* Vickie thought. Bridget Fallon and Vickie Fields lined up alphabetically in a straight line. The kind of coincidence that unwittingly leads to lifelong bonds.

And right behind us, Alex Fogarty. Pulling pigtails in grade school, snapping bras in middle school, and grabbing ass in high school. Catholic education was a pipeline. The kids you went to kindergarten with at Saint Regina's elementary school were the same kids you graduated from Saint Xavier's high school with. Your demons followed you from one circle of hell to the next.

But high school's supposed to be the end, Vickie thought. Her skin crawled. Vickie couldn't tell if it was melting snow running down her jacket, or just the idea of reuniting with people she gladly thought she'd never see again. The two of them plowed onward, but Vickie couldn't shake the feeling that they were really going backwards.

They finally reached the side door. The one leading from the cafeteria to get out for recess. Bridget knocked loudly.

"That's it?" Vickie asked. "Shouldn't there be a code? Knock three times, wait, knock two more times?"

Bridge tried to shoot her a dirty look, but it quickly dissolved into snickers. "What are we even doing here?" she asked.

"Meeting your bbbooooyyyffrrriieeennddd," Vickie sang.

There was a loud *clank* as the old door mechanism turned. Bridget elbowed Vickie. "Shhhh!"

Chris Castellano pushed the door open.

He's bigger, was Vickie's first thought. Chris' teenage bulk had been refined into sculpted muscle that stood out clearly underneath a plain black sweater. His hair was still cut short, little more than stubble, but he had the head shape for it. His face looked roughly worn for someone so young, but in a way that made him seem rugged and appealingly world-weary. The skin was taut along his brow and the flesh around his eyes seemed permanently shadowed. It blended well with the dark brown of his eyes.

Vickie supposed she could see the appeal.

Bridget and Chris looked into each other's eyes.

"Hey," he said.

Bridge smiled back. "Hey."

And just like that, they disappeared. Vickie could see the flat, cardboard replicas they'd left behind, but their essential selves had disappeared right before her eyes. Bridget and Chris had vanished into a private dimension all of their own, and they'd left these pale imitations as placeholders while they were gone.

She's so gorgeous, Chris thought. Bridget's skin was flushed from the cold and her eyes were clear and shining, magnified behind her glasses. She smiled at him, her shoulders up by her ears, and he was dying to kiss her. Bridget arched forward, just a little. Her mouth partly open. Just like the first-

"Shut the door! It's fucking freezing!"

Just like that, they returned from their pocket universe. Chris jumped back, letting them step inside.

Vickie came out of the cold and into her elementary school cafeteria. The room was lit by a smattering of LED lanterns instead of the overhead fluorescents. Vickie heard a propane heater blowing in the corner instead of the wheezing furnace rumbling in the next room. Other than that, everything was exactly the same. The same grey linoleum floor. The same cement block walls painted the same murky blue. The same popular kids gathered around the same cheap particle board lunch table. The details had changed a little, like specialty skins in a video game, but Vickie had no trouble recognizing any of them. Alex now had a regrettable attempt at a goatee and a puka shell necklace around his neck. Even in December, his face was bronze and there was a sand swept quality to his dirty blonde hair and Vickie just knew, *knew*, that he lived somewhere like San Diego or Hawaii and would inevitably find an excuse to brag about it within the next fifteen minutes.

Pete had gone the opposite direction of Chris. In high school, Pete's nickname had been Peterbilt 370 because of the way he could run through an opposing team's defense. But he hadn't been good enough for college, and the Peterbilt had run out of gas since Vickie had last seen him. The running back's cast iron body had atrophied under what looked like an extra thirty pounds of fat, and his tightly shaved crew cut had unfurled into an unruly afro. Pete's varsity t-shirt had been replaced by a AKA fraternity shirt and Vickie noticed an Alpha symbol actually branded into the dark skin of his arm.

Ellen seemed the least changed. She dressed like a stuck-up PTA head when she was nine years old, and she was dressed like a stuck-up PTA head now. Her body had just made a little more progress towards catching up to her inner forty year old.

Good progress, Vickie had to admit. The blonde was long and lean. Her jeans and sweater were not so tight as to be obscene, heavens forfend, but Ellen clearly had nothing to be ashamed of.

Except for the fact that her Facebook was regularly plastered with Young Republican Party talking points. Really spoiled what was otherwise an excellent presentation.

Tommy Baker… Aw, Jesus. Was that Tommy? If so, the ugly duckling had never made it into a swan. He was short, and his hair was greasy brillo. His eyes were too small and his lips were too rubbery. That was a cruel and shallow thing to think, Vickie realized that, but the kid she remembered was hardly kind or deep. Alex, Pete, and Chris were all assholes, but Tommy Baker was the only one who was a complete piece of self-centered, misogynistic shit through and through. And the naked way his eyes crawled up Bridget's body and then down Vickie's told her that not much had changed in that regard.

The other difference was on the tables. Instead of juice boxes and Chips Ahoy, the table groaned under the weight of two thirty racks of beer and an impressive array of liquor bottles.

Alex lifted his can of beer when he saw them. "Yo! St. Xavier's Class of '13 reunion!"

"Fuck that!" Pete piped up. "OG Saint Regina's 2007! Bring it in!" He started towards them, arms outstretched, but then the table behind him lurched forward, spilling beer everywhere, and the Peterbilt 370 himself stumbled forward and dropped on his face.

"Yeah!" Alex crowed. Pete's shoelace was tied to one of the table legs, and Alex strummed the taut lace like a guitar string before stomping over and jamming a finger in Pete's face. "Told you, Peterbilt! I told you it was game on!"

"Ignore them," Chris said to Vickie and Bridget. "They're in the middle of Prank War…. six, probably."

Rolling her eyes, Ellen stepped around Pete's prone bulk and greeted them both with an old lady hug, leaving forward so only their arms and shoulders actually made contact. "It's so great to see you guys again," she gushed.

Next she's going to try and sell us skin care, Vickie thought.

Chris appeared beside them with two cans of Bud Light. "Beer?" he asked.

"I'll take one," Bridge said.

Christ handed it to her, trying not to grin like an idiot as he did. He offered the other can out to Vickie.

"Vick?"

Vickie crossed to the bar table, leaving the beer hanging. She poured herself a slug of whiskey and knocked it back without flinching.

"I'm good," she said.

<u>6</u>

The Damned Fra Anjelico heard the colors below. He was a full floor above them, but the stone walls and steel stairwells allowed for excellent acoustics. Their laughter and cheer carried up as easily as if he were in the very next room.

They celebrated below. In the silence of his heart, the Fra celebrated with them.

Faith had sent the Fra to this place. He'd woken up with the name in his skull. *Saint Regina*- a seed planted in his mind by the Carcass God.

Saint Regina.

The Fra had the name in his head, and he had the inspiration in his heart- a pounding pulse assuring him that now, *this night,* was the night that he ascended in the service of The Grave.

The Fra had dressed in the black garments and the white shroud of Service. He had come to this place and waited for hours in the bitter cold. He had waited alone, his breath dancing in white swirls. He did not eat. He did not drink. He simply waited. Never doubting that, eventually, he would be put to use.

And now, Vindication. Their laughter and flesh was Infernal Promise fulfilled. They were the supplies sent to him by the Decayed Hand. They were proof that the Carcass God had seen the Fra's first kill, had seen Its servant spill the boy's blood by the fence, and had found it good.

The laughing flesh below, they were an omen that the Fra's Great Work could begin.

The Fra began to whistle, but stopped just as quickly. Music was blasphemy, not at all like the True Art he was about to embark on. He knew better. He knew the magnitude of the task set before him. *How do you expect to succeed if you lack the discipline to even begin properly?* He chastised himself.

He needed to clear his mind. The Fra closed his eyes.

The fires disappeared. His blades disappeared. The corpse in front of him disappeared. Behind his closed eyes, all was darkness. All was empty.

In the darkness, only one thought remained- the only thought that mattered.

The Mural.

The Fra held his breath. Seconds passed in blackness. Then a minute.

Still, in his mind there is The Mural and only The Mural. He does not feel the ego at being chosen by The Decayed Hand for such a great work. He does not feel the eagerness to begin his craft.

The need for air felt like water rising in the Fra's chest. And then in his throat. Breath strained to get out of him. The Fra held it.

In the dark, his focus is only on what the work represents. The Damned Fra Anjelico, for all the honor of his title, is nothing but a rotted fingernail on the decaying corpse of the Carcass God.

It was death he held in. To refuse breath was to reject life, and the Fra rejected it until his lungs screamed and begged behind his clenched lips.

I am Yours, my God. I am Yours. I am Yours.

Another minute passed. Two minutes. Three. The Fra felt his brains quiver in his skull. Brain cells turned cold and lifeless.

Slowly, with no great urgency, The Damned Fra Anjelico let the breath out. His lungs cried out for deep, gulping breaths, but the Fra was strong again. He forced himself to take small, shallow breaths, letting his flesh wallow in its state of deprivation.

Properly befouled, he could now resume his preparations.

In days gone by, this had been the art classroom. The large space with its long work tables was now the ideal studio for the Fra to create his masterpiece. The Fra picked up the large chopping knife. His reflection lurked in the flat silver of the blade. There was nothing to be seen of his face, everything but his eyes was hidden by the white canvas shroud he had become, but the Fra's eyes were enough. They blazed with rapturous joy- joy a Baptist preacher would have recognized from a mile off. The joy of a servant in pursuit of the Lord's work.

The Fra cut once. Cut twice. His hands moved gracefully now, not clumsy like they used to. The Decayed God had taught him skills. And strength. The Decayed God had bid him to cast aside his old name and take his place alongside masters like the Condemned Michelangelo and the Unrepentant Monet.

He made eight more cuts, pressing down on the wide blade with the manner of a housewife cutting celery sticks for company. It was clear that he had made no mistakes, but the Fra took a fastidious inventory of his work regardless.

They were all there as they should be. Ten severed fingers lined up by length in five neat pairs.

The Damned Fra set down the chopping knife and took up the straight razor. He started at the corpse's forehead and dragged the cutting edge all the way back beyond the corpse's ear. A defoliating shampoo couldn't have produced a more perfect result. The Fra cut exactly where hair met scalp, leaving the skull pristine and shearing off the long strands of lush, brown hair necessary for his own needs.

The Damned Fra Anjelico gathered his cuttings of hair and flesh and brought them to the fire. He had six aged, wrought iron braziers set atop two of the long tables. Small iron cauldrons rested atop five of the grates. Most of the fire pits were still cold and dark, but a low fire burned in the basin of the sixth pit. The Fra had prepared his fire the same way Infernal Artisans had prepared theirs for centuries. Chips of dried tarantula husks for kindling. Wood taken from graveyard trees for fuel.

It was by the orange light of the fire that the Fra began the next step. He took one of the severed middle fingers and held the severed stump over the glowing embers. He kept it there until the stub of bone turned black and the flesh began to bubble. Once the flesh was properly melted, the Damned Fra grabbed a clump of hair and carefully pressed it into the molten flesh. He scalded his own fingertips some, but that was irrelevant, the important thing was making sure the hairs set properly into the bubbling skin and that they were all the same length.

When the Fra judged his work to be satisfactory, he set the finger down to cool… and he picked up another one.

It was a pinkie finger this time. As such, the Fra used substantially less hair, bundling the bristles to a dark point little thicker than an eye pupil.

He felt a small pang of regret as he evaluated the skin of the severed finger. It really was a lovely shade of Butterscotch Cream. But the ritual was clear, and this flesh served a different purpose. The Fra set down the pinkie brush and picked up a ring finger. He repeated the ritual of flesh, hair, and fire. He repeated it seven times more.

With the ten brushes laid out before him to cool, he evaluated them one final time. *The servant with a crooked blade can only offend his Master.* That was from the Book of Revilements: chapter nine, verse nineteen. The Fra would not be a foolish servant. He would be meticulous. He would set to his craft with perfect tools and, therefore, he would offer his Master a perfect work.

The fingers were not bent. The bristles were properly congealed and set at the perfect lengths. The Fra said a small prayer of thanks. From the largest to the smallest, the brushes crafted from the flesh and hair of Todd Reed were flawless down to the most minute detail.

The Damned Fra returned to Todd's remains. He cut again with the straight razor, drawing the blade down the length of the corpse's sternum. The skin peeled away from Todd's chest with ease, but the bone underneath was not so compliant. The Fra took hold with both hands and pried upwards with all his might, but the corpse's ribs refused to acquiesce to his strength.

A frustrated snarl escaped from behind the shroud. This was not the way. The fragile skeleton should have easily come apart under his power. A lesson perhaps. A final reminder that the strength of life could never match the strength of death.

I have heard your teaching, my Lord. Now I beg you, grant me Your strength so that I may better serve You. The Damned Fra reset his grip in the gaps between Todd's ribs. His muscles bulged. His breath wheezed between gritted teeth. *Faith,* he repeated. *Faith.* He strained harder. The scars stood out along his forearms and biceps, as if underlining his effort in lines of white and pale pink.

At last, Todd's rib cage came open with a tremendous *crack*. Pieces of the rib clattered to the floor. The body jumped violently on the table. Blood splashed up, spattering the Fra's shroud in a red haze.

The Fra smiled. He felt the still warm blood soaking his face. *Praise to the Black Grave!* He knelt and gathered up the broken bones. Some had shattered into small curves of bone no larger than a kitten's claw. Others were mostly intact and longer than a pizza crust. It didn't matter. They would all serve a purpose as pallette mixers- thin, flexible pointed tools for mixing colors together.

Behind him, Todd's remains continued to steam- hot flesh escaping into the frigid room, but the Fra paid the body little attention now. His tools were ready.

Next, he needed to gather his paints.

In the cafeteria below, one of the colors laughed.

The Damned Fra laughed right along with them.

7

Vickie heard a loud *crack*. Probably a tree branch breaking outside. The wind was howling and the snow was piling up. A glance at her phone told her the forecast called for five feet by morning,

She couldn't believe that they were actually going to sleep here. Was there enough fuel for the heater? How were they going to get out if Pete's brother didn't answer his phone tomorrow? Were there any extra sleeping bags or were she and Bridget just supposed to shiver?

Not that Bridge would need her own bag. She was already cozied up next to Admiral Protein Shake as they set up their third game of beer pong. Twice now, Chris had lifted his hand but stopped just short of settling it on Bridget's lower back. Vickie didn't know what Chris had told his friends about them, but the situation should have been obvious to anyone with half a brain.

Of course, Tommy was currently pantomiming sex with an empty bag of cheetos, so who knew? Half a brain might be one system requirement too many.

"Let me get some of that?"

Vickie snapped out of her musings. Ellen was right beside her, with just a hint of extra shine in her green eyes. *She's buzzed for sure,* Vickie thought. "The vodka, I mean," Ellen pressed. Slightly impatient now.

"Right. Sorry." Vickie stepped quickly to the side, making a path for Ellen to mix herself a vodka and Sprite. Vickie expected Ellen to coast back to her pals, but the blonde lingered beside Vickie at the "bar" instead. "So, what's up?" Ellen asked.

Vickie shrugged. The way Ellen was looking at her, she felt like an interesting relic someone had dug up from the back of an attic. She lifted her cup and flashed it like it was proof of identification. "Just hanging out," she said.

"You majored in Liberal Arts, right?" Ellen asked.

"Graphic Design," Vickie corrected. "With a minor in education."

"That's right. You were always hanging with that hippie art teacher," Ellen said. "That's cool. You know what you want to do and you don't care if you're not going to make any money. Sometimes I wish I could do that."

Vickie bristled. There was an insult there- buried like a razor blade in an apple. She forced herself to ignore it.

"I've actually got a job in marketing. I'm working for a boutique firm in Charleston that does direct mailers, promo posters- that kind of stuff. There's a lot more freedom to do what I want than in the big agencies."

Ellen leaned in close. Vickie smelled the alcohol coming off her in waves. She also smelled a hint of passion fruit, but Vickie did her best to ignore that too. "Let me ask you something," Ellen whispered. "Do you think Chris and your friend are *fucking*?"

Vickie kept it cool. She sipped her drink. " I don't think so," she said. Which wasn't technically a lie. Vickie assumed that Bridget wouldn't have kept it from her if she was sleeping with somebody.

"I think they arrree," Ellen drawled with a scandalized grin. She swayed a little. Obviously the alcohol was affecting her equilibrium as much as it was tugging at the edges of her dignified sensibilities.

It wasn't doing jack shit to her powers of observation though. Vickie supposed she wasn't surprised Ellen had figured it out. She and Vickie had been in honors courses together in high school. During junior year they'd taken part in a very spirited debate over legalizing gay marriage. Vickie had argued her case with a passion that she hadn't quite understood at the time, but she nevertheless came away with a grudging respect for the blonde's agile mind.

"If they are, then he's a very lucky guy," Vickie said. "Bridge's the best."

"Are you speaking from experience?"

"...What's that supposed to mean?" Vickie asked.

"You know," Ellen said, wallowing in the insinuation like a pig in shit. "You…. Her…. *You.*"

With some effort, Vickie restrained herself from emptying a drink on the judgmental bitch's head. Instead, she cast her eyes at the sausage party around them. "Alex… Chris...Pete… Tommy…. *you.* Hopped on any trains lately, Ellen?"

Her reaction. Oh, Vickie wished Ellen would hold still long enough for Vickie to immortalize it in a portrait.

"You don't have to be a bitch," Ellen spat. "It was just a question."

"Well, the answer's no," Vickie said.

Ellen backed off. "Whatever," she mumbled, and rejoined the group next to the beer pong table. Tommy tried the ol' "hand on the lower back" move himself, but Ellen deftly stepped out of his grasp.

Vickie poured herself another drink. *How many is this? Four? Five?* Whatever, she needed to put a few layers of anesthesia between herself and this shitshow.

"Vickie!" Bridge shouted. "Get over here! Celebrity shot!" She waved Vickie over to the table, the same table where she was beaming ear to ear with her hulking fella by her side.

Sellout, Vickie thought, and then pushed that poisonous thought as far down as she could. To prove it, she jogged over to the table and accepted the plastic ping pong ball. Even though she hated this fucking game.

"Come on," Bridget cheered. "You can do it!"

"You got this," Chris said. He patted her on the shoulder, like he'd never called her a freak or laughed along when his friends scribbled a giant penis on the front of her notebook.

Vickie cocked her elbow. God help her, she even made the effort to aim before she threw it. No matter, her shot sailed wide over the table, onto the floor, and rolled all the way to the double doors and out into the dark hallway beyond the ring of the lantern lights.

"Oh!" Pete lamented. "So close. Tough luck, Chris. You wasted your celebrity shot on the one lesbian that can't pitch."

"I wouldn't worry too much, Bridge," Vickie snapped back. "You're still playing the only black guy that can't ball."

Vickie was mortified the second she said it. *Oh my fucking Christ.* If there'd been a mirror in front of her, she would have expected to see some asshole in a red MAGA hat looking back at her. Vickie's jaw hung open- to say what, she didn't know- but Pete started laughing first. In point of fact, Pete doubled over and pounded the table. His eyes were shut tight but his mouth yawed wide in a paroxysm of laughter. He wasn't alone. Alex was laughing too and so was Chris. Only Bridge seemed to share any of Vickie's mortification.

"Ohhhh," Pete wept. "OH! That was a good one." He straightened up. "Woo! Gonna need some snow for that burn!" He jogged off in the direction of the ball.

"Watch out for Sister Keller!" Alex shouted after him as Pete disappeared into the darkness of the hallway.

Chris laughed. "Oh shit, I remember her."

Bridget jumped in, "She was like a ninja! She'd just pop up-" Bridget twisted her hand into an arthritic claw and clamped onto Alex's shoulder. "Who said you could use that phone young man?" she wheezed in a passable impression of the old crone.

The others laughed together. Vickie did not. All she remembered was a withered bitch who constantly criticized Vickie for everything from her "immature" interests to the "sloppy" way she wore her hair.

"Ah, those were the days," Alex lamented.

"Days run by a bunch of nuns and sexless biddies who may as well be nuns," Vickie said. "I'd rather be down on the peninsula in Charleston any day."

Alex perked up. "No, shit? That's where you ended up? My macro firm has an office there. I thought about transferring, but Oahu is just so fucking stellar. But I get you- way better to be around beach and babes than here, amirite?"

Under the beer pong table, Chris' hand edged towards Bridge's. She gratefully squeezed it.

"Did we lose Pete?" Ellen asked.

"Yo!" Chris shouted. "Petey!"

The only response was his own voice echoing back at him from the dark hallway.

"Petey!"

"-etey!"

"-ey!"

"...He's fucking with us," Aex said.

"Or he's passed out," Chris added.

Alex took the remaining ball from the water cup and lined up his shot. "I'm gonna take both shots," he said.

"...Is nobody going to check on him?" Vickie asked.

Chris shrugged. "And do what?"

"He's retarded," Tommy said. "He's either waiting to sack tap the first person who comes through the door or he stopped to take a piss and he's passed out with his dick out. No thanks."

Fine. Vickie let it drop. Not like it was her friend. She mixed herself another whiskey and coke. *What happened to the last one?*

Whatever. She wasn't driving.

Something shrieked out from the hallway- a rattling cacophony of ugly sounds crashing against each other. Vickie jerked, dousing her hand in cold whiskey. The sound came again, making them all look in the direction of the door. The rhythmless *cha-chunk* raged in Vickie's head like a wasp hissing in her ear. "Jesus, what the fuck is that?!"

Ellen rolled her eyes. "That would be Peter."

The sound rattled on again, roaring from the dark. Less startling, but no less unsettling. It clattered on like a railroad from the beyond.

"That's Pete?!" Vickie asked.

"If there's something stupid and loud to do, Pete will find a way to do it," Chris assured.

"It's okay. Take it easy, Vickie," Bridge said.

Anger surfaced above Vickie's unease for a moment. Was Bridget really telling her to *calm down?*

Alex groped for his phone. He squinted at the screen, trying to make his bleary eyes focus. Finally, he pawed at the screen and his cellphone light flashed on.

"Let's see what the dumbfuck is doing."

Unwillingly, Vickie cast her eyes towards the door leading to the hallway. Alex's light was already there. The doorway wasn't dark anymore. Vickie saw the familiar linoleum and block walls, but it didn't make her feel better. There was no sign of Pete. Just the empty hall.

It looks like a trap.

"I'm gonna stay here," Vickie said.

"Me too," Ellen added.

The ghastly clattering sounded again. A midnight train.

And then Pete screamed. He howled from the darkness beyond Alex's light.

"Pete!" Chris yelled. He took off running after his friend's scream without a second thought, outracing Alex's flashlight and plunging into the darkness.

The clattering and the scream had scared Bridget, but they didn't stamp on her heart like this. The sounds weren't nearly as horrifying as watching Chris disappear like that.

He could never come back.

The thought sprung into her head, instant and complete.

He Could Never Come Back.

Bridget sprinted into the hallway. And Vickie, shit, Vickie ran right after her like they had magnets in their asses.

Pete screamed again. It was even louder here in the hallway. Alex and Tommy had joined in behind Chris and the others. Alex's shaky light danced ahead of them as they ran, but it wasn't Alex's epileptic light guiding their way- it was memory. They were all alumni. They knew where this hallway led, and they knew the path to follow in their muscles. It had been ingrained there over eight years of school. The cafeteria leading to-

Chris shoved open the final set of double doors and burst into the gym. Adrenaline flooded his system. He was dimly aware of the others behind him, but his only concession to their presence was to place himself slightly in front of Bridget. The only thing that mattered was finding Pete.

They poured into the gymnasium, Ellen had joined them, unwilling to be left alone in the cafeteria. Alex's cellphone light swung across the cavernous space in erratic arcs. It illuminated the basketball hoops and the bleachers. It shined over a trail of blood. A long, spattery rope of it wound across the wooden floor of the basketball court- glistening black in the pale blue light.

"Holy shit," Ellen murmured.

Finally, the light fell onto Pete. The Alpha Kappa Alpha alumni lay flat on his back with his hands over his face. Blood fanned around his head like the glory of Christ in a stained glass window.

They crowded around him. Chris got their first. He knelt beside his friend but stopped short of touching him, wary of aggravating some injury. "Pete! What the fuck happened?!"

Pete took his hands away from his face. Vickie winced. Tommy retched and took a big step back. "Jesus Fuck!" Alex shouted. Pete's bottom lip was split completely in half. Blood was still gushing down his chin. Bridget knelt down beside him. She ripped her scarf off and pressed it over Pete's mouth.

"Stay still, okay, Pete?" she said with remarkable calm. "Just stay still."

Alex leaned in close. Half giggling and half revolted. "Dude, how did you fuck yourself up this bad?"

Muffled by the scarf, Pete's mouth moved regardless. "Ahm a Thortido!"

"What did he say?" Ellen asked.

"Oh, Jesus Christ," Chris moaned. He had his light out now too, but he wasn't aiming at Pete. His light was focused on the corner where the trail of blood had originated. Caught right in the center of the beam, just beyond the blood, a two foot square of neon yellow plastic lay upside down with its four cheap, plastic wheels sticking up in the air. Vickie hadn't seen one of those in years, but she recognized it immediately for what it was.

Third grade. The same gym, only lit by fluorescent lights overhead and sunlight pouring in from the tall windows on every wall. Coach Ruddell blows the whistle and the eight year olds are off. Twenty of them in the same red shorts and white t-shirts, scuttling around on those little neon plastic scooters, batting a puck around with tiny hockey sticks like hand sickles.

Vickie is hopeless. She doesn't have the coordination to balance her butt on the scooter and shuffle her legs along with any kind of speed. Tommy hits her from behind and bumps her off the scooter. Alex runs over her fingers. "Speed bump!" he yells, just in case there was any doubt he did it on purpose.

Meanwhile, off in a world of his own, eight year old Peter Arrogate kicks off of the wall with as much force as he can muster. The boy rockets forward, lying flat on his stomach with his arms tucked tight to his side and his legs stretched out straight behind him.

"Torpedo power!" he shouts as he careens across the floor.

"Thortido Pawher!" Pete shouted, muffled by the scarf. He raised his fists triumphantly as if he were bench pressing an invisible barbell.

Chris panned across the gym with his light. There was a whole stack of plastic scooters in one corner. There were soccer nets, a sack full of dodgeballs, and a large stack of rubber gym mats.

"It's all still here," Chris said.

"All part of the sale," Alex put in. "The diocese wants to squeeze every penny that they can out of this place. There's gonna be an auction."

"Who's up for a game?" Tommy asked. "Dodgeball? Soccer?" He winked at Ellen. "Shirts versus tits?"

Ellen ignored him. She helped Pete sit up. "He needs to get stitches," she said.

"Not tonight he's not," Vickie said. She was looking up at the window, snow still buffeting the glass in a torrential haze. On cue, a strong gust of wind rattled the old panes.

"Maybe some snow would help though," Chris said. "Keep the swelling down." He held out his hand. Alex threw him the keys.

Bridge didn't volunteer to go with him, that would have been too obvious, but while the others were still focused on Pete she drifted away and slipped out after Chris as the double doors closed behind him.

She hadn't told Chris that she was going to follow after him. She didn't need to. He was there waiting for her in the dark. The shadows hid his features, hid everything but his essence. He was just strength and urgency rushing towards her. His hands grabbed her around the middle, molding to her hips like they were forged for that exact purpose. He lifted her, light as a dream, and pressed her hard against the wall.

Bridge went willingly. She wrapped her legs around his waist. She pulled his face tight against hers. They kissed, mouths opening and closing in perfect sync. Her smell, clean hair and fresh gingerbread, filled his head.

"I've been waiting to do that all night," Bridget breathed. Chris responded by smashing his lips against hers again.

He'd done well for himself ever since puberty-cheerleaders, gymnasts, swim team. But there'd never been anybody like this. Nobody had ever cut him loose from his body and left him swimming in euphoria like this nerdy, sweet, hilarious, beautiful girl that he'd ignored for years like an idiot. He kissed her as a substitute for words he hadn't been able to figure out yet.

I need you.
You're the best thing that's ever happened to me.
I love you.

"I've got to tell you something," he said.

"I do too," Bridge said. She pressed something into his hand. Something small, square and wrapped in foil.

"I don't want to wait anymore," she whispered. "Later? Tonight?"

Chris nodded. He slipped the wrapped condom into his pocket, and then he kissed her again.

Anything else he had to say could wait.

\- \- \-

They came back with two red cups filled with snow. The others had moved Pete so he was sitting up against the wall. He still had Bridge's scarf pressed against the bloody gouge in his lip.

"Here," Chris said. He held out a cup. "Get some of that on there, brotha."

Pete cheerfully complied. The others winced as he pulled the scarf away, but Pete seemed completely unbothered as he scooped snow from the cup and pressed it against the valley of blood in the center of his face. With his free hand, he offered out Bridget's scarf for her to take back.

Bridget took one look at the bloody rag and stepped back. "That's alright," she said. "You keep it."

And then she smiled. The need to smile kept creeping up on her. She tried to grab Vickie's eye. She wouldn't need to speak, a single look would tell her everything Bridget needed to say.

Except she couldn't. Vickie stood at the back of the group, looking pointedly out the window and not even paying any attention to Pete or the rest of them.

"You only brought a drink for Pete?" Alex asked. "That's bullshit, man."

"I think we ought to tone it down a little before somebody splits their skull instead of their lip," Vickie said.

Alex swung towards her. He swayed a little to cope with the sudden shift in fluids running through his system. "You're one to talk," he finally slurred. "I've been pushing just to keep pace with you all night. Damn girl, I didn't even know you drank back in high school.

Vickie folded her arms. "I didn't. Some of us just didn't peak at sixteen."

"You're a fucking beast is what you are. That's all I'm saying." He set off back towards the cafeteria. "I'll be back!" he cried.

Tommy stood up too. "Wait up. Ellen- gin? Vodka?" He bowed. "I'm at your service."

"I prefer my service like Amazon," Ellen said. "Impersonal."

Tommy's solicitous smile disappeared. In its place was something far uglier. His lip twitched, but he said nothing.

Alex had not waited up. Alex was already gone. Tommy hustled after him anyway.

"If he had a tail, it'd be stuck between his legs," Vickie muttered.

Gratefully, nobody else heard her. Bridget slid over to Vickie's side. "They're only going to think you're kidding for so long," Bridget said in a hushed tone. "If you keep acting like a bitch, someone might eventually decide that you are one"

"Wouldn't want that," Vickie whispered back.

"What's your problem? *They like you.* There's no reason to keep acting like an asshole."

No reason, Vickie thought. Bridge spoke as if the casualty of their cruelty made it more forgivable. *"Nothing personal,"* said the boy to the daddy long legs, *"I just felt like pulling the legs off something."*

"Please, Vickie," Bridget pressed. "Tonight's important to me." Bridget looked into her eyes and that was enough. Vickie got it. Got *why* tonight was important. She sighed. Bit her lip.

"Hey, Chris! Come help me with this," she said loudly. She went to the stack of gym mats and grabbed one by the corner.

"What're you doing?" Chris asked.

"Safety," Vickie said. She grunted, struggling to get some traction with one of the heavy rubber mats. "We obviously can't be trusted on the hardwood floors."

Chris joined her. Working together, the large gym mat came down with ease. They dropped it onto the floor and then went back for one more.

"Hey, Vickie," Chris said in a low tone as they pulled side by side. "I don't know if you remember, but back in high school, in the library, I was kind of a dick to you that one time."

Vickie tugged harder at the gym mat. "Yeah, I seem to remember more than one time."

It was too dark to tell, but Chris flushed red. "Yeah, you're probably right." They hauled the second mat down and went for a third. "I get it if you don't like me, but I'd like to make it up to you if you'd give me a chance."

"Don't make it up to me," Vickie said. They dragged a third mat down. For the first time, she actually looked him in the eye. "Make it up to Bridge." Vickie spread her arms wide and dropped down on her back. "Ah," she sighed loudly. "Much better."

Bridget needed no formal invitation. She dropped down next to Vickie, reclining on one arm like an Egyptian princess. "Mmm, yes. This will do," she giggled.

"Okay, okay, everyone stand back," Chris said. He launched himself forward into a cartwheel with stunning agility. His shirt slipped down at the top of his arc, revealing a brief glimpse of abs like cobblestones before he flopped down next to Bridget. His eyes met hers. He had time for one brief, satisfied smirk before a dodgeball squished his nose with stinging force.

"Gameh Onh!" Pete shouted through his swollen face. He was on his feet and searching for another dodgeball, his split, clotted lip no more bothersome than an errant speck of dirt.

He's still hurt, a mature voice in Chris' head cautioned. *If you wing one back at him, you could open his face back up.*

Very true. Best to hit him in the balls then, the same voice concluded.

Chris didn't need a second consideration. He wound up and pegged his best friend between the legs as hard as he could. Pete doubled over, groaning and laughing and already reaching for another dodgeball.

The dam broke all at once. Bridget, Ellen, and Vickie scrambled for the sack full of dodgeballs and retreated to separate corners of the gymnasium, flinging wild shots at each other as they separated. Vickie had not thrown a ball since she realized she could get out of gym by claiming to have cramps, but she dove into the game with gleeful gusto. She pegged her best friend in the ass and cackled gleefully at Bridget's outraged whoop. She aimed for Chris' chest, struck him in the face instead, and almost meant it when she yelled out, "Sorry!"

It didn't take long for Alex and Tommy to return, arms laden with beer and liquor. They took a moment to absorb the chaotic cloud of flying dodgeballs, and hastily set down the alcohol and took up their own ammunition. "Oh, it's on, motherfuckers!" Alex shouted. Tommy cocked his arm back. "Torpedo this!" Tommy shouted. He struck Pete in his ample stomach. The legendary Peterbilt Truck doubled over. First he was laughing, but his gasping chuckles soon devolved into ugly retching. He stumbled to the side, still clutching his stomach.

"Yo!" Alex yelled. "Yo! If you're gonna boot, do it in the bathroom. I'm not cleaning that shit up." Still unable to speak, Pete flashed a thumbs up. He lumbered towards the double doors, hand clamped over his mouth.

Slinging rubber at each other, the rest of the party barely noticed.

8

Pete shuffled through the pitch black hallway like a salmon returning to its old spawning grounds; muscle memory guiding his path back to the bathroom he'd gone to every day for eight years. There was no time to wait for his sight to catch up- not with his guts churning and the taste of Hot Pocket's past bubbling at the back of his throat. He stuck his hand out into the darkness and was rewarded with the sensation of an old wooden door creaking open. Pete lurched inside. A burp seeped from between his clenched fingers and made his own nostrils curdle. He took two bounding steps, then a third, and that was all she wrote. Vomit poured from Pete's throat like garbage from a split bag. His stomach convulsed and he poured a second helping of beer and dinner slurry between his feet.

Pete remained doubled over; hands on his knees for support and sucking air through his mouth. His heaving breath boomed in the closed confines of... the bathroom? Hopefully?

Had he really made it to the bathroom? And if he had, had he managed to reach a toilet? The darkness around him was complete. For all Pete knew, he might have just poured a load of puke all over the custodian's office. Alex would be pissed, but... c'mon. That would be pretty funny.

Pete groped for his pocket and took out his phone. He keyed on the flashlight app and the first thing he saw was a ceramic tile wall. He recognized the faded green from eight years of bathroom breaks and two or three smuggled cigarettes with Chris and Tommy. Job well done, he'd made it to the bathroom.

Making it to a toilet was another story. In his blind rush, he'd dropped a payload of vomit on the floor squarely between two urinals.

Eh. Good enough.

He brought his fingers to his face and they came away wet and steaming red and beige in the flashlight beam. He spun around in search of the sink and instead met with a white shrouded face looming directly in front of his. The figure's dark eyes burned lumescent black in the flashlight's glare.

Oh shit!

Pete tried to shriek, but nothing came out except for a dull wheeze. He tried to recoil from the masked face, but his legs merely twitched. The 367 Peterbilt called out to his body for action and received nothing in reply. He floated in the bathroom like a pickled thing in a jar.

Pete's head dropped down on a neck that would no longer support its weight. Staring down the length of his torso, he saw two thin knives sunk into his chest. The blades had slipped cleanly between his ribs and into his lungs; so sharp and so narrow, Pete had never felt a thing.

His killer lifted him up, lifted him by the knives buried in his lungs. Pete felt pain then. It erupted deep within him, burning away his drunken haze and leaving him writhing in agony like a worm on a hook.

But he still couldn't cry out. Even knowing the brutal truth, knowing that his life was being taken from him while he stood by in agony, he could only take in and out faint, hissing breaths like air seeping from a tire.

The Fra pushed his victim against the wall. His hot breath rebounded off the shroud, moistening his lips. The Fra marveled at the lightness of his offering. The strength of the Grave surged through him. The boy twitching at the end of his knives was full of color and yet he felt as light as an empty bucket.

The Damned Fra waited. Watched. He did not blink. He kept his rotted brown eyes fixated on Pete's rapidly greying features.

That was the Way. The Fra waited as, slowly, something dwindled in Pete's pupils as he suffocated. Something intangible, but definitely there. The Fra watched it grow smaller and smaller until, at last, it was completely gone.

The Fra pulled his blades free. Pete's remains crumpled to the floor, but very little blood dribbled out. The Rotted Hand had guided his knives straight and true. It was a sign They were pleased with his preparations.

I swear, my Lord... Your guidance will not be put to waste. The Fra hefted Pete's carcass up by the waistband of his pants and hauled the body down the hall, carting the weight along easily with only one massive hand.

9

Well, this worked out for the best, Vickie concluded as she flung a side arm shot across the gym. She didn't have to talk to anyone, but Bridge was still happy. Her new "friends" seemed to be enjoying themselves too.

And Vickie? Vickie got to work out her aggression without being so overt about it. It was therapeutic really.

Also, it was a helluva lot of fun.

They'd spread more mats out until almost the whole floor was covered. The better for pulling off ridiculous, uncoordinated leaps through the air. The six of them ran and leapt through the gymnasium, little more than shadows tinted orange by the streetlights outside as they flung dodgeballs at each other with reckless glee. Vickie panted and wiped sweat from her eyes. She lingered to the side, watching Chris sprint after Alex, waiting for him to wind up... release... NOW!

Vickie leapt into the air. She flung the ball at the top of the arc, grinning with satisfaction as the ball hit Chris in the air and rebounded into the air with a healthy *BONK*.

She never saw the collision coming. Ellen, laughing and dancing away from Alex, stumbled into her path.

"Look out!" Vickie screamed.

It was too late. Vickie collided with Ellen. They fell to the floor with unnatural perfection. Vickie sprawled on top of Ellen, her hands on either side of the blonde's head and one leg flung over her hip. Ellen's hands clutched Vickie's waist, holding her in place.

….And it was fucking electric. They slotted together like a plug into a wall socket. Vickie's eyes met Ellen's and, Jesus Christ, *she felt it too.* The unexpected moment had left Ellen bare. Vickie saw it all- surprise, and then want. The hands on Vickie's waist squeezed tighter for a fraction of a second. The blonde's lips parted. She tilted her head.

And then Ellen was awkwardly scrambling out from underneath her, the hunger in her eyes replaced by panic.

"Sorry," she mumbled. She wiped her hands on her pants. "I'm gonna go get a drink."

Vickie watched Ellen retreat to the cluster of bottles by the door and pour herself a very tall cup of straight gin. *Which was more than you could say about the very tall blonde drinking it,* Vickie thought. Christ, Vickie wondered how she hadn't seen it a mile off. Classic, repressed little-

Hypocrite much? Vickie chastised herself. *Ellen's a fucking stranger to you. And is a stranger supposed to have an opinion about another stranger's sexuality? NO, they are not. Leave it alone.*

Yes. That was all well and true and good.

...Still, the idea of Ellen becoming less of a stranger seemed a lot more interesting than it did a few minutes ago.

Ellen took a massive gulp of gin and lowered her cup with shaking hands. She raised the cup again, only to have it snatched out of her hand. The sloppy grab splashed liquor down the front of her sweater. Clammy moisture seeped through the wool to clutch at her chest.

"C'mere, El," Tommy slurred. He crouched down in front of her with three bottles tucked under his arm. "I've got just the thing for you." Without bothering to empty the gin, he carelessly began adding ingredients to her cup. A splash of vodka. Some tequila. A liberal pour of Mountain Dew Voltage. With some effort, Tommy rose up from his squat and offered the cup back to Ellen. He leaned in close, totally blind to the way Ellen recoiled from his offering. "You know what they call this?" he whispered. "A panty dropper."

Vickie knocked the cup out of Tommy's hand, splattering blue liquid all over the gym, and placed herself squarely between him and Ellen. "Thank you, Tommy, for proving that you know as little about mixing drinks as you do about talking to women or brushing your fucking teeth."

....It took Tommy a minute. His beady eyes narrowed to a hateful squint. "Nobody... nobody's talking to you, dyke."

"Nobody's talking to *you,* failure." Vickie shot back. One of the dodgeballs was at her feet. Vickie bent down to pick it up and stood with much greater ease than Tommy had managed. "Why don't you just take this, back off Ellen, and go back to playing with yourself. I'm sure you're used to it."

Tommy's lip curled in a sneer, but he said nothing. He just glared at Vickie, who stared right back at him with supreme indifference. The blue ball that she'd picked up still hung in the air between them, waiting for Tommy to take it from her.

He slapped it from her hand. "Fuck you," he muttered sullenly before storming away. Vickie watched him go, savoring a warmth in her chest that had nothing to do with alcohol.

"Yo, Tommy!" Chris shouted. Tommy didn't turn around. He didn't even break stride or look back as he shoved the doors open and disappeared into the hallway.

The warmth in her chest was gone, but Vickie stood her ground, even as Chris came up to her. "What the fuck was that for?" he asked.

"Welcome to life after high school," Vickie said. "Assholes get called out now when they don't leave girls alone."

"He's just being an idiot," Chris said. "It's not a big deal."

"Not for you it's not. You don't have slimy assholes shoving shitty drinks in your face because they don't know how to take a hint."

"Yeah? Well, anytime you want to take a hint, Fields. You know where the fucking door is." He brushed past her.

"Chris!" Bridget shouted. He ignored her. The booming echo as he slammed the door behind him was Bridget's only answer. Bridget swung back towards Vickie. Vickie resisted the urge to look away from Bridget's reproachful gaze. She was right. What did she have to apologize for?

"Tommy's his cousin," Bridget said. "They're best friends." And then she was off and running after Chris, not caring what anybody thought. Vickie, Ellen, and Alex stayed behind, off-kilter points of a triangle. Drunk, remorseful, and confused.

"....Truth or Dare?" Alex ventured.

"I'm going back for the whiskey," Vickie said. With luck, she could get numb enough to walk home.

<u>10</u>

The Fra returned to the art classroom with the first of his paint buckets. He threw Pete's corpse onto one of the long tables, letting the cadaver's head dangle off the edge. The Fra selected a scalpel from his satchel of tools and set one of the cauldrons on the floor underneath Pete's head. The pot was heavy, black iron. It seemed to suck in the light around it, a black void amongst shadows.

The Damned Fra made two expert cuts underneath Pete's chin. The result was instantaneous. Fresh red paint poured from the twin wounds, gushing into the iron pot in an ever growing pool of Garnet Red.

When the flow waned to a dribble, the Fra set the cauldron aside and swapped his scalpel for an obsidian skinning knife. Six inches of black glass honed to an edge as thin as an eyelash.

The Fra would not sully this blade with cloth. He used his bare hands to rip the shirt and jeans off the carcass. The sight of the undraped flesh made the Fra shudder with pleasure.

It's perfect, he thought.

He glided the knife over Pete's chest. The skin peeled off easier than a window decal, coming away from the flesh without even a whisper of resistance. The Fra cut Pete's skin away in long strips and brought the pieces to the second pot. He'd had the fire burning for fifteen minutes, and the water was bubbling ravenously. The Fra added the tangled knot of skin. The boiling water darkened with blood, but that wouldn't last. The blood would burn off. So would the water. The skin, soaked soft, would not evaporate. It would melt- first to jelly, then to a clumpy soup, and then, at last, to a fine, velvety paint.

The Fra watched the skin, already beginning to liquefy in the basin. If he only had two eyes, it might have been difficult to tell the skin's color in the murky light from the fire and the streetlights, but the Fra saw clearly with the third eye gifted to him by the Carcass God. He knew the bubbling mass would bloom into an excellent shade of Alcazar Brown.

He gave thanks to the Decayed Crown for blessing his preparations.

His color palette was developing nicely.

11

"Tommy!" Chris shouted. "Hey, man! Come on!" He walked down the hallway with Bridget at his side, flashing the light into every empty classroom.

Mrs. Langan's old room.

Mrs. Platt's room.

Sister Mary Helen's.

They saw the desks lined up like mourners at a funeral. They saw the snow drifts climbing ever higher up the windows. Chris didn't talk, but Bridget heard his breath churn in the gloom. She took his hand, but he didn't squeeze back. It felt like she was holding a wrapped hunk of steak from the butcher.

"Vickie can be prickly," Bridget said.

"You're a poet and you don't even know it," Chris said. He tried to smile but his mouth merely twitched like a dying snake.

Bridge forced a laugh. "No, Todd's the poet. I told you about him."

"Maybe you should have brought him instead," Chris said.

"Vickie's just used to hanging out with a different kind of crowd."

"Lesbos and weirdos?"

Bridget stopped walking. She pulled her hand away from his.

"No," she said. "That's who I hang out with."

Ah, shit, Chris thought. "I'm sorry, Bridge. That was an asshole thing to say,"

"That's a shitty poem," Bridget said.

Chris reached for her hand. She stepped back.

"Come on," he pressed. "I said I was sorry. What else do you want me to say?"

"That would be cheating, wouldn't it? You tell me, Chris. What do you want to say to me?"

"Don't give me that shit, Bridge. That's not what we do."

"You're right, it's not. But I've never seen you around your friends before. Maybe this is what you do when they're around," Bridget challenged. "I told Vickie you were different-"

"I am different," he tried to say, but Bridget kept talking right over him.

"-But maybe you're still just a jock asshole like your friends."

"You're wrong."

"About what, Chris? I wish Vickie would drop the attitude, but I know where it's coming from. I just thought we weren't in that place anymore. But if my best friends are still freaks, does that mean I'm still a freak? If so, then what's a bigshot frat boy like you-

"I wasn't in a frat!" he erupted. His belligerent roar bounced off the stone corridor and surrounded Bridget from all sides.

"Chris, I didn't mean-" Bridget began.

"I wasn't in a frat, ok? I'm not hopping down to New Orleans for March Madness. I don't have a condo in Hawaii. I'm not even a fighter. I'm a personal trainer that they used to hang out with." He turned away from her before she could answer. He went to the nearest classroom and shoved the door open.

Chris looked out over the empty desks, dimly lit by the light from outside.

This was Mrs. Dallo's room. Fourth grade.

Even then, Chris was already the biggest and the strongest kid in class. Always one of the team captains in recess. Pete, Tommy, and Alex were already his best friends. They were completely inseparable... except for two hours after lunch. That was when Pete and Alex went to the "Apex Room" for special classes while he and Tommy stayed behind with the kids who weren't as smart.

Bridget came up behind him. "Vickie's always telling me how much she loves Charleston," she said. "She's always talking about how much she loves her job, and her neighborhood, and what she's doing with all her new friends... she's never coming back."

"You could move there," he said.

"She told me that too. But what am I going to do? Waitress? Bartend a night shift while she goes to happy hour with her work friends? I wouldn't have the same life as her. I'd just be like… some keepsake she brought from home. And that sucks. It really, really sucks." She took his hand. This time, it really felt like his hand. He laced his fingers in with hers.

Chris sighed. "Every time I see them, I feel like it's going to be the last time. Tommy's the only one I talk to more than once or twice a month."

"I know I'm just a waitress," Bridget said, "But if your friends are half as smart as you say they are, I don't think they're going to let themselves lose touch with you."

"They're idiots," Chris said. "They're just good at counting. You're the one that can relax. Vickie seems smart for real. No way she's letting you go."

"She'll have to let me go a little bit," Bridget said. She cupped his face and turned him so he was looking at her. "Because I'm not going to Charleston. I'm not going anywhere without you."

He wrapped his arms around her waist and pulled her tight against him. She came willingly.

"Bridget. Being with you…" he began.

"I know," Bridget whispered. "I feel it too. It's… it's ours."

He pressed his lips to hers. Their mouths worked together with urgency, trading breath and desire. She dug her nails into his chest. He trailed his hands down her back and squeezed just below her ass. He lifted her and Bridge let herself be carried. He brought her into the room and dropped her down on the teacher's desk. She felt the frigid metal through her pants, but it didn't matter. Not with Chris' lips roving down her neck. She separated from him just long enough to pull her shirt over her head, and then clutched him close to her chest.

The stupid bra she had on underneath was from Victoria's Secret. It was the most expensive bra she'd ever bought. It had been humiliating to ask Vickie to detour so she could get it, but after she put it on she'd been satisfied that the effect was worth it.

She didn't even think about her bra now. Chris didn't notice it either. He simply buried his face in her cleavage and kissed his away across the small swell of one breast. Bridget moaned. She waited to feel his hands at the clasp between the cups of her breasts.

Chris was feeling the same need, and he would get there soon enough.

First, he needed to reach into his pocket for what she'd given him earlier.

12

Vickie sat *(sulked)* in the kitchen. She sat on the serving counter, resting her back against the cold iron of the industrial oven. Except for her phone, the darkness here was complete. Vickie hunched over its blue glow, as comforting as a twilight campfire in hostile country.

She didn't have to be back here in the kitchen. The cafeteria was empty now. Vickie could have sat in an actual chair and had the whole place to herself if she wanted to.

But the school kitchen had been one of their hideouts growing up. The school only served hot lunch as a Friday treat. The kitchen was cold and empty the other four days- the perfect nook for reading or playing on a DS, provided you weren't afraid to slip past the lunch monitor at recess.

Vickie took a pull from the bottle. Jim Beam offered a different type of escape than Pokemon Pearl, but it sure didn't suck.

A shriek whistled from the cafeteria. Vickie didn't lift her head from her Tumblr feed. The wind did that every ten minutes or so. She didn't even bother checking the forecast anymore, she had it down by heart. Snow, snow, and more snow. All the way until the morning light.

A morning I'll be greeting with these fucking idiots.

The drink wasn't helping as much as she thought. And the Tumblr scene was totally dead. Vickie sighed. Refresh. Refresh.

Something in the dark slapped hard against a cement wall. Not the wind. Vickie sat up. She peered in the direction of the door but saw nothing there but oily curtains of darkness.

"Who's there!?" she shouted. She swung her phone light in the direction of the door, but the pale blue light fell on nothing but an empty doorway. Vickie swallowed. She told herself there was no reason for her heart to pound like this, no matter how many horror movies she'd seen with this exact scene. Horror movies where the idiot shouts "Who's there!?" just before someone pops out of nowhere and cuts their fucking head off.

"It's Christmas, not Halloween, assholes! If someone's out there, say something now."

And if it's Tommy I'm gonna beat him to death with this fucking bottle.

She waited. She heard nothing except the sound of her own breathing. She held her breath in a bid to eliminate the distraction, but she could still hear it. Thin, shallow whispers of air. In and out. In and out.

Oh God...That's not my breathing.

Vickie took a step back. She tried to still the pounding of her heart so she could hear better. Yes, there was no mistaking it- she still heard someone else's fast, jittery breath in the darkness.

The lit phone in her hand suddenly felt like a signal flare. She switched it off and slid a foot backwards, silently as possible. Even in the pitch darkness, she (thought) she knew the way to the back exit. She tried to step softly, not giving away her movement. Maybe she was just being paranoid, but they'd all been drinking and the boys were all *Genus Frat-us.* That was reason enough not to be alone with any of them.

"Vickie?" a voice hissed. A pregnant pause. "Vickie, are you in here?"

Vickie recognized the voice. It did nothing to slow her racing heart.

Oh shit.

"Yeah," Vickie said. "Yeah, I'm here." She fumbled her phone back on and searched for the flashlight app.

Be cool. Be cool.

Vickie still wasn't sure she believed it. This was a trick of the wind and too much Jim Beam. But she turned on her phone light and, sure enough, there she stood.

Ellen Cutter.

She really was beautiful, even in the sterile blue light from the cell phone. Willowy and graceful, with high cheekbones and a perfect bow of a mouth. There was a hesitant friendliness on her face, incredibly different from her usual haughtiness and amazingly humanizing. Under different circumstances, Vickie would have loved to ask her to stay like that for a quick sketch.

But these are not those circumstances.

Oh no, they definitely were not.

They stood across the kitchen from each other. Vickie tried to act casual, and she seemed to be doing about as good of a job as Ellen was. The blonde awkwardly hefted the bottle of gin. "I was getting tired of boys," she said. Her face flushed black in the flashlight's blue glow. "I mean, Alex," she said hastily. "He's waiting in the gym so he can 'sack tap' Pete after he finishes throwing up. They're so dumb."

Vickie hopped up on the metal counter. Plenty of room if Ellen wanted to join. "Well, you're in luck because I happen to be very smart. Three point three final GPA."

Ellen snorted. "Three point six"

Add those together and you've got six point nine, Vickie thought, but didn't nearly have the brass to say. Still, Ellen hopped up beside her. Not right next to her, but close enough to test the waters. Vickie warmed up a little. She was no Ruby Rose, but she knew how to make another girl feel comfortable. Under the right circumstances, that could be enough to make things interesting. "So, how's the wild west?" Vickie asked. "You're in law school, right?"

"Yeah," Ellen said. " I thought about looking at some other schools, but UT offered me a huge scholarship. I couldn't really say no."

"So no plans to come back to PA?" she asked. As they spoke, Vickie casually shifted a little closer. Just close enough that their arms grazed. Vickie felt a tingle run across her skin and nestle in the back of her neck

Ellen felt something too. Vickie saw it in the way her eyes got bigger as she took another sip of gin. "No, I don't think so. Austin has a lot more going on." She fidgeted in place, pressing her arm a little more firmly against Vickie's.

"Not too liberal for you?" Vickie teased. She was talking a little too fast. Nervous energy.

"Just because I'm conservative doesn't mean I can't live in the world, Vickie," Ellen huffed. "I like Austin just fine."

"I guess it's still Texas, right? Can't be too hard to find a church and a gun."

Ellen actually laughed. "You got a problem with the Bill of Rights?" she joked. She bumped Vickie with her elbow. Vickie shoved her back playfully... and she let her hand fall on Ellen's thigh. Just to see what would happen.

Ellen kissed her.

To be frank, Ellen swept over Vickie. She assaulted the brunette with explosive vigor, relying on sheer enthusiasm to compensate for what she lacked in experience. Vickie reciprocated eagerly. She clutched at the back of Ellen's head and licked the taste of gin off of her tongue. She matched Ellen's enthusiastic pace, but she didn't lead. She let the novice blonde move at the pace she wanted.

Ellen wanted to go fast. She pushed Vickie flat on the steel table and slung one delectable thigh over her waist. Vickie had the briefest glimpse of Ellen's face- lipstick smudged, her sensible hairdo mussed up like she'd been caught in a hurricane, and then Ellen dove down and attacked the brunette's neck with her lips and teeth.

Stinging tingles raced down Vickie's spine. There would be marks tomorrow for sure, but Vickie didn't care. "Yes," she moaned. "Fuck, yes. Keep doing that." She felt Ellen's hands next. They started low at Vickie's hips and crawled up her torso like trails of liquid fire until they squeezed her breasts. The touch came over her shirt, but it was still enough to make Vickie writhe in ecstasy.

She grabbed Ellen's face and pulled the blonde away from her neck and into another forceful kiss. Ellen groaned. The hands fondling her breasts moved faster. Still kissing her thoroughly, Vickie went to return the favor. She slipped her hands under Ellen's shirt, fingertips luxuriating against bare skin and shoving Ellen's bra out of the way before closing her hands around the petite buds of her chest. Vickie cupped Ellen's breasts. She had time for one thought- *My god, they're perfect*- before the warm flesh abruptly retreated away from her grasp... followed all too quickly by the rest of Ellen.

The blonde scrambled off of the table and yanked her sweater back down. Vickie sat back up, feeling the molten heat in her stomach collapsing into cold pig iron. "It's okay, Ellen," she said.

Ellen's eyes were wide. She clenched and unclenched her hands at her side, backing towards the door without ever taking her eyes away from Vickie. Maybe she thought she was actually speaking, but all she did was open and close her mouth like a fish underwater.

Vickie tried to shrug, like Ellen was speaking with perfect clarity. In a way, she couldn't have been clearer. "It's okay," Vickie repeated. "It's not a big deal. You had a couple drinks and just...

But she was only talking to herself. Ellen was already out the door. "Shit," Vickie whispered. She went for the Jim Beam, desperate for another slug of whiskey.

The bottle was empty.

-　-　-

Ellen ran down the hallway, away from the cafeteria and away from the gym. She ran away from heated breath and from the hands she still felt branded into her chest. She ran through the darkness and stopped abruptly as her shin slammed into a step in the darkness. The stairs. Ellen grabbed the bannister and followed it up through the night. She took the steps in twos and threes and finally stopped running as she reached the second floor landing. There, Ellen doubled over against the guardrail, clinging to the icy bannister and trying to ignore the memory of the warm body she'd embraced only moments ago. Her heart pounded, her breath came in ragged gasps, and none of it had anything to do with physical exertion.

She'd always believed that she was focused. That she was driven to succeed. That's why she found it so easy to turn down dates in high school. That was why she'd spent her Saturday nights at the library instead of frat parties during undergrad.

Except it turned out that wasn't why at all. The "why" was waiting in the kitchen with beautiful black hair and the softest lips Ellen had ever felt. Vickie's touch had brought that truth crashing down all at once, and Ellen had recoiled from it. It was too much. A whole sea change that Ellen couldn't process at the same time that Vickie was grinding against her.

And yet, running hadn't changed anything. That truth was still in front of her face. Panting and shaking, Ellen couldn't deny that she wanted it.

Don't quibble. Say the words.

Yes, that was the truth- Ellen still wanted *her*. Desire, real, red-hot desire surged through her, pulling her body taut like a bow string demanding to be let loose.

Alone in the dark, Ellen could admit that. She wanted Vickie Fields. That changed a lot about who she thought she was. It left her shaken and incredibly confused.

….But whatever may have changed, there was at least one thing about herself that was still the same: Ellen Cutter always went after what she wanted. She knew what her mother would say. She knew what the Church would say. She knew what the Young Conservatives said. She held everything she'd ever been taught her in the palm of her hands… and she let it melt away as easily as snow brought indoors.

"I don't give a shit," she whispered. "I don't give a shit!" she said louder, and her voice echoed back on her in the black stairwell. Ellen laughed out loud, suddenly buoyed by a lightness she'd never felt before. She wheeled around, hoping Vickie would still be in the kitchen. Still waiting for her.

She nearly ran right into the shadowy figure standing behind her. Rough hands grabbed her arms.

"About time you showed up," Tommy slurred.

Ellen tried to pull back, but Tommy's fingers fastened into her biceps and held her in place. She could barely see him in the windowless stairwell, but she could smell the alcohol wafting from his body on every breath.

"I was starting to think you weren't coming," he said.

"Tommy, come on-"

"But I knew that was bullshit." He pressed her backwards until Ellen felt the cold stair railing against her back. The scent of vodka only got stronger, and she could feel his rancid breath against her face now. Tommy's clammy hands squeezed her chin. "I knew sooner or later you'd come for that panty dropper."

"Oh, my fucking God, *stop!*" Ellen snapped. She pushed him hard. Tommy was completely unprepared for it, Ellen caught him in the torso, forcing the air out of his lungs. He doubled over, gasping. Ellen stood over him and wiped at her face, as if the residue of his touch were still there. "I'm going back downstairs," she said. "You can do whatever you want."

Tommy's hand was a blur in the darkness. It was a glancing slap, catching her mostly on the neck instead of the face, but it still made her teeth ache and sent her reeling sideways.

"Whatever I want?" Tommy hissed. "That suits me fine." His shadow surged towards her.

"No!" Ellen shouted. She felt real fear for the first time. She tried to push him away, but Tommy's stringy body only pressed harder against hers. It was not just his hands now. His reeking lips assailed her face. His thigh pressed between her legs. He pinned her against the guardrail.

"Help!" Ellen screamed. She struggled against him. She managed to get her back away from the stair railing, but Tommy still clung to her like a leech. "Chris! Alex! Get him off me!" She struggled to break free from his squirming fingers. "Vickie!"

"Oooo, getting kinky now," Tommy oozed. He took his hands off her arms and moved them to the hem of her pants. "I could get into that."

Ellen snapped her knee up. With Tommy trying to straddle her, his crotch was wide open. She struck him square in the balls, mashing them high against his body.

Tommy squealed. "Oh, you fucking cunt!" he screamed.

Ellen grabbed Tommy by the shoulder and flung him to the side.

All she meant to do was push him out of the way. Truly, that was it. Even consumed by fear and revulsion, all Ellen wanted to do was put some space between herself and Tommy. Just enough space so she could run back to the others. Over the next few minutes, Ellen would repeat that to herself time and time again.

I just wanted to get away.

But in the dark, she had no real idea which way she was pushing him. And Tommy's equilibrium was already reeling from the shots of liquor and the shot to his testicles. He tumbled against the guardrail and didn't even try to grab for the railing. He simply tumbled over the bannister, like a kid doing a flip off the high dive, and disappeared from sight.

"Oh my God," Ellen gasped, but she couldn't even hear herself over Tommy's trailing scream as he fell.

But she heard the echoing crunch as he landed on the stone floor below.

13

"I'm an idiot," Chris said.

Bridget, buckling her pants, grinned. "Ouch," she said.

Chris smiled back. He took her hands. Kissed her fingertips. "Not you. Never you. I mean Tommy. Let's go back and find the others. Tom can come out of hiding whenever he gets tired of being a jackass."

"You wanted to make sure he's okay," Bridget protested. "There's nothing wrong with that."

"He is okay. Vickie's right. He's got to learn not to act like an idiot. Besides..." he turned away, but not before Bridget saw the grin split his face. "What?" she asked.

"...I want to tell them," he said. "My friends. Your... Vickie. Let's tell them we're together."

He turned back towards her, expecting to see her smiling. Maybe even a little teary-eyed. Instead, she surveyed him with a skeptical tilt of the head. "I don't know. You're kind of below my level. I mean, I've got like, eighty followers on Tumblr. I can't-"

That was as far as she got before, laughing, he lifted her off of her feet. Bridget shrieked with laughter and cradled his neck as he carried her and pressed her against the coat closet. They were kissing again, falling deeper into each other and losing touch with the cold metal and wood around them.

Too soon, Chris broke the kiss. He held her in his arms, savoring her smile and the warmth of her things in his hands.

"I'm sorry for how I treated you in high school," he said. "I was an asshole."

She smirked at him. "Obviously, I got over it."

"I'm serious," he insisted. "I don't know why I was like that. And not just to you. To anybody."

"You didn't mean it," Bridget said.

"That doesn't make it better. Maybe if I'd been less of a dick... maybe I would have found you sooner."

Bridget waggled her eyebrows. She kissed his shoulder and worked her way up his neck with excruciating slowness.

"Wellll," she drawled. She punctuated every sentence with a nip at his pulse. "If you're really. Really. *Really* sorry... I know how you can make it up to me."

She pulled at the hem of the shirt he had just put back on.

We can tell everyone later, Chris reasoned. Nobody was going anywhere.

- - -

Dead.

Vickie sighed. She knew it was coming, but that didn't make her feel any better about the worthless brick her phone had become. One feed update had finally been one update too many. She was truly alone now, cut off from the rest of the world by a dead phone and four feet of snow on every side.

And inside?

"People say Hawaii's expensive," Alex droned on, "But that's bullshit, because *anything* that's worth having is expensive. What really matters is making sure you that the value is there for the cost. And I know you get it, Vick. The beaches. The climate. The miles between you and any asshole you don't want to see. You can't put a price on all that."

Couldn't agree more, Vickie thought. She hadn't replied to a single one of Alex's many, *many* proclamations about the virtues of South Pacific life, but she could drink to that one. She knocked back another shot of vodka. The alcohol had finally gotten away from her. She was well and truly drunk now. Drunk and getting drunker, heaping fuel on the simmering fire growing hotter and hotter in her gut.

I can't believe I'm with these fucking idiots again. She'd gotten away. May 29th, 2013- here's your diploma Ms. Fields, and here's a letter certifying you never have to see any of these assholes ever again. We'll forward your ten-year reunion invite to the nearest trash can.

Vodka. She'd kept that promise in college and onwards and upwards into her professional life. No frat boys. No sororities. No more toxic masculinity. Just guys with blue hair and girls with no hair; '80s punk rock fans and '90s sci-fi fans. And gay people. Actual, real life fucking gay people.

No snow warnings in South Carolina, but she'd holed up with friends during torrential rain storms, and nobody smashed face-first into a wall like a fucking toddler. They talked about movies or played Cards Against Humanity. She'd been alone with her friend Ashley during one of those storms, and *she* certainly didn't run away screaming the first time she kissed another girl.

Rum. Yet, somehow, here she was with the same idiot meatheads she'd happily outgrown. No, not somehow. She knew exactly how. Bridge. Bridget Teresa Fallon. Bridge, who had somehow settled for the stupidest, meatest head of them all.

Gin. No, not Gin. SoCo. Where was Bridget anyway? They couldn't still be looking for that fuckboy Tommy. No, she was probably off seeing what steroid abuse had left between Chris' legs.

Vickie snorted out liquor and snickered to herself.

Tequila. She needed to get Bridge away from here was what she had to do. Too much time in Pine Hollow did something bad to your brain. Vickie had only been back a day, and she already felt it working at her nerve endings.

Ah, speak of the happy couple! Bridget and Chris had returned to the cafeteria. Jesus, they were actually holding hands.

"Yo!" Alex shouted. "What took you guys so long? Is Tommy still holed up somewhere?"

"Don't worry about him," Chris said. "Can you guys come here for a second? Where's Ellen and Pete?"

"Pete's out there waiting for me to let my guard down, probably with a whole garbage can full of snow. No thanks. I'm staying right here."

"And Ellen's got women's troubles," Vickie slurred. She sensed Bridge trying to make eye contact and pointedly ignored her.

"I knew she was ragging," Alex said.

"It doesn't matter. We'll tell them later," Chris said. He shifted awkwardly from one foot to the other. "I just wanted… I mean, we. *We* just thought that everybody should know that Bridget and I…" he squeezed her hand tighter. "Well, I didn't invite her here tonight because we're friends. We're dating. And Bridge..." he favored her with a smile that was positively radiant. "She's incredible."

He looked expectantly to his friend. There was a moment's shock, but not a long one. Alex came forward like a proud grandparents entering the delivery room. He clapped Chris hard on the back. "I wish I'd known you had true love sitting in history class when you were carting around that bitch Jen Borton all sophomore year!"

He moved to Bridget next, flinging a friendly arm over her shoulder. "Okay, you're gonna need to know a few things about my boy here. He drafts too many long shots in fantasy football, so you have to make him rein that in. And don't let him drink 151 after midnight. Bad things happen." He gave her a companionable shake that rattled the teeth in her head.

Bridget heard Alex and Chris still talking, trying to include her, but it was Vickie that she sought out. Beaming, Bridget turned towards her best friend.

And Vickie, flashed a grin that looked as positive as a nun's pregnancy test, sardonically toasted her, and kept to her lonely spot slouching against the far wall.

Bridget reluctantly let go of Chris' hand. She slipped away from the happy clamor and went to Vickie just as she finished the last of the vodka in her cup. Even from three steps away, Bridget caught the reek of alcohol coming off of her. "Vickie, are you okay?" Bridget asked.

"Vickie? Or do you mean Barb?" Vickie hissed. "I can't believe you left me alone with these fucking idiots."

Bridget ignored the insult and touched her friend's wrist. "Did something happen while I was gone?" she asked.

Vickie bit her lip. She didn't keep secrets from Bridget, but this was Ellen's secret, not her own.

"No, nothing happened," she said. "I just lost a couple IQ points listening to Alex explain why 'Mahi Mahi' really needs the extra 'Mahi.'"

"If somebody did anything to you, tell me," Bridget persisted. "I'm not going to let anyone mistreat you. Chris won't either."

"I don't need protecting, Bridget."

"Then what's your problem?" Bridget asked.

"I told you. I don't have a problem."

"So you're just being a bitch then?"

Vickie reared back. She wouldn't have been rocked harder if Bridget had punched her in the mouth.

"Nobody's been anything to you," Bridget continued. She didn't yell. She just pressed on in the calm, matter of fact tone of someone reading the farm report. "Everyone's treated you like normal," she said. "Better than normal, actually. Nobody else is carrying their high school grudges around."

"Oh, so gracious of the popular kids," Vickie shot back. "Really big of them not to hold the fact that they treated us like shit against me."

"Will you fucking quit it!?" Bridget erupted. "I'm sorry we're not all as cool and evolved as your new Charleston family, but I'm going to have a good time. If you want to be a bitter fourth-grader again, that's your business."

She turned and walked away before Vickie could get a word in. Her best friend, walking away with her shiny dyed hair and new glasses.

Going to sit with the cool kids.

Bridget kept her chin up and her stride steady. Alex and Chris were staring at her. God, they must have heard everything.

Bridget pretended that they hadn't. She took a beer from Alex and tried to ignore the way she was shaking. "Thanks, Alex," she said. Something inside her stomach scratched at her with a thousand spindly legs. Her teeth ached. Hot pressure squeezed behind her eyes.

Chris put an arm around her and squeezed her close. "Alex," he said. "We can't make it out with you guys on New Year's Eve, Bridge has to work. Is it cool if we catch up with you at the ski house on New Year's Day?"

Bridget's busy on New Year's Day, Vickie thought. *It's the Carrie Fisher marathon.*

But if Bridget even remembered, she certainly didn't say anything.

"Hell yeah, man," Alex said. "My dad already said we can use it."

"Cool," Chris said. "You're gonna love it," he told Bridget. "We go every year and it's always a blast."

Alex laughed. "Your boyfriend is the greatest show on skis," he said.

Chris jokingly shoved him, even as Bridget laughed along. "Don't you join in with him," Chris warned, but he grinned as he said it.

Meanwhile, Vickie took one step towards the hallway. And then another. And another.

Nobody noticed. Least of all Bridget.

Whatever, Vickie fumed. She began to pump her legs faster. The floor was rocking beneath her feet, but she managed to maintain her balance and keep on forging forward. The double doors and the black hallway beyond it looked more and more inviting.

If Bridget wants to get knocked up and mix his protein shakes, that's her business. I've got my own fucking life. Vickie pushed the door open and was met by a bone white face stepping out of the blackness.

Vickie didn't even recognize Ellen at first. The blonde's eyes had doubled in size. More striking than that, something had been ripped out of them. Her brightness had dimmed. The ever-present sharp intelligence and cool assuredness in Ellen's eyes was just... gone. Blasted out of her.

"I just wanted him to leave me alone," Ellen murmured.

Vickie opened her mouth. To comfort or question, she didn't know and would never find out. The ungodly mixture of alcohol flooding Vickie's system finally caught up with her. She doubled over and threw up all over both of their shoes.

14

Mark Fogarty was going to murder his son.

He stood behind the desk in his home office, a beefy man who shaved his head regularly. A man with a nose streaked purple with broken blood vessels and a smile built for dirty jokes and football chants.

He was not smiling now. He was carefully counting the keys in his lock box; counting because he was a careful man who was aware that he had a temper. Counting because it was entirely possible that he might do something in his anger that he would not be able to undo. Better, therefore, to be certain of the facts before he made any decisions that he couldn't take back.

His wife, Sheila, waited in the bedroom with bated breath. She was afraid of what her husband might do, but knew better than to try and get in his way. They'd come home early because her migraines were acting up. She would have stayed at the hotel, but Mark had said that if she was going to complain, then she could do it at home instead of in a six hundred dollar a night suite.

So they'd driven back through the relentless storm, twice nearly skidding off the road and once narrowly avoiding a head-on collision with a snowplow. Sheila had screamed then. Mark had only tightened his grip on the steering wheel. "Scream in my ear again, Sheila. Please. If you do, I swear to Christ I'll leave you on the side of this fucking road."

She lay there on top of the comforter now, listening to his breath hiss through his deviated septum and wishing dearly that she'd just taken the pill and tried to suffer through her headaches in silence.

...Eleven. Twelve. Thirteen.

Thirteen. Thirteen keys. One was missing. One missing key to Saint Regina Academy... and one missing son.

"That little shit," Mark muttered. "That sneaky, lying, underhanded little cocksucker."

"Mark?" His wife called timidly from the bedroom.

"Shut the fuck up, Sheila!" he roared. "Take your Imitrex and go to sleep before I shove the whole fucking bottle down your throat!"

Somewhere, on another planet, the bedroom door squeaked shut. Mark barely heard it. His attention was already back on his son. The boy had run wild in high school- cops once or twice. A situation with a girl resolved in a way that the Pope wouldn't have approved of. Mark had tolerated all of it to a degree, but he'd sat Alex down the night after he graduated from college. He'd poured them both a glass of 20-year-old MacClellan scotch and explained a couple facts of life to his young man.

"Fuck around time is over, son. I don't expect you to be a priest, but I expect you to know where the line is and I expect you to stay on the right side of it. If you can't, if you find yourself covered in shit that you can't wash off, I'm not lifting a finger to help you. You live with the smell like a man."

And did breaking and entering cross the line? Did stealing from your own father count as keeping your nose clean? What about undoubtedly wrecking valuable real estate with your numb-fuck friends? Was that over the line?

Oh, yes. It certainly was.

Outside, the wind shrieked like a boiling tea kettle. It was one o'clock in the morning, and the plows had just about surrendered the fight. The snow was still coming fast and furious. The roads looked like unplowed paths in the Siberian tundra. Despite his steely facade, Mark was well aware that they'd been lucky to make it home, even with his big Range Rover.

The boy has to come home eventually. You can break his neck just as easily tomorrow morning.

Yeah, but how many windows would be broken by then? How many drunk retards would take a shit in a classroom before daybreak? How many hours would his son, his own flesh and blood, sit there giggling, so proud of himself for pulling one over on his old man?

Was he really going to let the boy laugh it up all night like there weren't going to be any fucking consequences?

Mark's choice was clear. His boy, an underhanded weasel with underhanded motives in mind, had stolen the key to the back entrance. Mark, a righteous man of integrity driven by righteous purpose, took up the key to the front entrance of the school.

He put in the pocket of his parka along with the key to his Range Rover.

15

"Shit," Alex repeated. Not for the first time. "Shit. Shit. Motherfucking shit."

Nobody answered him. He'd said pretty much everything there was to say. All the rest of them could do was follow behind his bobbing flashlight beam in a single file line.

None of them particularly wanted to go, but nobody wanted to be left behind either.

"It was so dark," Ellen had said. Her voice as shell-shocked as her eyes. *"All I did was push him away from me. I didn't know that the railing was there. Then he was screaming…. And then he wasn't."*

It was bad. That much, they all knew. And, deep down, they all knew how bad it really was. Tommy was dead. He was fucking dead.

But Ellen couldn't, or wouldn't, say the word. She talked about the push. And the fall. And Tommy's still, dark husk on the floor as she staggered back to the cafeteria, but she wouldn't say the "D" word.

So now… this. This dark procession down the hall, lit by Alex's flashlight and accompanied by his constant muttering curses.

"Holy fucking…. Jesus fucking…. *Shit!"*

Chris and Bridget followed behind him. Bridget had one hand on his arm and rubbed slow, soothing circles between his shoulder blades as they walked. Occasionally, she murmured something low that Vickie couldn't hear.

Vickie followed a little further back, coaxing Ellen along like an invalid. The blonde truly wasn't with them anymore. She could recite some details of the incident if you asked, but she had become like a resource desk. There wasn't a person there anymore. There were just facts and figures.

Vickie wanted to feel furious, except there wasn't anybody there to be angry with, was there? Tommy had fallen.

"Oh, shit."

It wasn't Alex this time. It was Chris. They had come to a stop. The murky outline of the stairs was there in the outer aura of the flashlight's beam. Alex, Chris, and Bridget had clustered together in a gloomy line, obscuring Vickie's view of anything there was to see at the foot of the stairs.

"This is good, right?" Chris said in a shaky voice. "It means he's okay."

"Chris…" Bridget warned.

"I don't mean *okay*, but Ellen made it sound like he… I'm just saying, this might not be a bad sign."

Cautiously, Vickie stepped away from Ellen. She made her way up to alongside Bridget and the others. She was still braced for the worst, no matter what Chris was trying to convince himself of, but she still wasn't prepared for what she saw.

Tommy was not there.

His blood was. There was a massive pool of it on the floor, a red stain the size of a welcome mat, and there were some small, white flecks floating in the red pool-

Oh Christ, those are his teeth.

But there was no body. There was only a steady trail of red leading back up the stairs. Up towards the second floor.

Chris pointed at the bloody path marks. "Look. He walked away"

"But why would he walk *away* from the cafeteria?" Bridget asked.

"Because obviously he's fucked up," Chris said. "He's hurt and… confused. He doesn't know where he's going. We've got to go get him."

Bridget took out her phone. "We need to call an ambulance."

Alex ripped the phone out of her hand. "Hang on. Let's think about this a minute."

"Hang on!?" Bridget asked. "Do you see how much blood he's lost? He needs a doctor. Now."

"We'll call Pete's brother," Alex said. "He can dig us out, and we'll take him to an emergency room."

"Alex, that could take hours. Give me my phone."

"Listen. Do you have any idea what my dad's going to do to me if a fucking ambulance comes here?" His face looked exceedingly pale in the flashlight's glare, and he couldn't stop licking his lips.

"We'll figure it out, Alex," Chris cautioned. "Bridget's right."

Bridget reached out towards his clenched hand. "Give me my phone,"

"I said we're not calling anyone!" Alex yelled. He flung the phone against the wall, smashing it in a starburst of broken glass and plastic.

Chris moved before the pieces had even finished falling to the ground. He pinned Alex's wrist against the stone, pressed a forearm hard against his throat, and bared his teeth in a doberman snarl.

Vickie didn't move any slower, she was just further away so Chris was able to get hands on Alex first. That didn't mean Vickie had any intention of stopping. She cocked her fist back and aimed over Chris' shoulder for Alex's nose.

Bridget pushed past Vickie before she could throw the punch. She shot her friend a warning glance and then gently touched Chris on the shoulder. "The priority right now is Tommy, right?" she asked. "Let's find him and we can take it from there, okay?"

Vickie reluctantly let her clenched fist fall. Chris made no such move. His forearm stayed tight against Alex's throat. He was almost nose to nose with his friend, his lips still twisted in a snarl. "I'm okay, Chris," Bridget said. "It's Tommy we need to worry about. Right?"

"Fuck," Chris said. He ripped Alex's phone from his hand and turned it towards the stairs. Spatters of blood, black in the phone's glare, led up the steps. "Come on. Let's hurry up."

Ellen shook her head at the sight of the trail leading to the second floor. She made a muted squeak of protest and took a step back into the shadowy confines of the hallway.

"I'll stay with Ellen," Vickie said. She drifted back towards the blonde. She kept her hands to herself, but she stood reassuringly close to the trembling woman.

Bridget nodded. "That's a good idea. We'll be back soon."

"Yeah," Vickie said. She met Bridget's eye. In that moment, the fight they'd had in the cafeteria seemed like the absolute stupidest thing in the world, and Vickie was sorry for it. Thankfully, she didn't need to actually say so. She knew that Bridget could see it in her eyes. "Be careful," she added.

"Little late now," Alex muttered. Chris gave him a shove. "Let's move," he said.

The three of them made their way up the stairs, the light from Alex's phone fading as they rose.

Eventually, it was gone completely.

16

The Damned Fra ran with no regard for concealment or stealth. He had to trust that the Carcass God would make it so the other colors would not hear his echoing steps and heavy, panting breath as he ran back to the studio with the leaking can of Chantilly White.

Precious Garnet Red oozed from the broken body. That was bad, but there was plenty more red to be found. The real problem was the skin. The quality of the paint was degrading by the second.

It shouldn't have been like this. The Fra had been there, lurking in the shadows at the end of the hallway and growing ever closer as the Chantilly White argued with the Blush Rose. They were both too caught up in their emotions, her fear, his lust, to have any idea that the Fra was coming closer by the second. The Decayed God was truly with him then. The Fra's every step was silent as mold creeping over a corpse. He had his hand spike at the ready- the long, thin iron spike that was the ideal tool for swift, bloodless death. He had his angle of attack prepared. Two single thrusts, right through the crown of the skull, and both colors would be his.

The Fra was moments from the first strike, and then the Blush Rose pushed the Chantilly White over the bannister. The Fra cried out. He couldn't help himself as the Chantilly spilled down and out of sight. Doomed providence be praised, the Blush Rose screamed so loudly, the Fra's own cry was not heard.

She ran down the steps before the Fra could even think to grab her. In hindsight, that was a blessing. In his fury, the Fra might have damaged the Blush Rose too. In point of fact, the Fra might have smashed the Blush Rose's face against the bannister and might have kept smashing it until she was nothing but an abstract art exhibit splattered across the hallway.

It was better this way. The Blush Rose and the other colors were trapped by the snow; none of them were going anywhere. Better that the Fra try to salvage as much of the Chantilly White as he could.

The Fra barreled into his studio and threw the corpse onto his preparation table. In the flickering light of his fires, the damage made the Fra want to weep. Wasted blood overflowed off the table and puddled on the floor. The impact had turned entire sections of skin an ugly, mottled Blueberry Jam. Other parts had turned January Snow as blood loss bleached away the skin's natural hint of red. *Wrong. All wrong.*

No. He could save it. Through the will of the Carcass God, all things ruined and discarded could be brought to glory. The Damned Fra Anjelico himself was proof. He had been less once. Then, he had discovered The Faith. He had learned the power of the Carcass God. The Decayed God had taken the Fra's raw meat and turned it into something greater. The Fra would do the same here.

The Fra went to work with the skinning knife. He peeled Tommy's Chantilly skin away in jagged, irregular chunks. The smashed head was useless, riddled with bits of broken skull and stained grey with brain matter. The chest, not much better. The Fra hacked at the boy's back, arms and legs. When he was done, the pitiful amount of Chantilly he'd salvaged barely filled half a pot.

If half a pot of Chantilly is all you have, then half a pot is all you were meant to have. The Faith didn't come to you when you needed it. The Faith came when It needed you.

That was The Way. The Damned Fra thought back to who he once was, to the wretched excuse for a man that he'd once been. That man had looked upon the strength of others and felt only bitterness and resentment. He had complained. He had bemoaned his fate.

Lost. That was what he was, lost and searching for a voice to come out and give him a purpose.

The Fra watched his meager supply of Chantilly White boil in the pot. One hand unconsciously went up to his neck, under the shroud, and fingered the rippling scar left behind by the rope he'd tried to hang himself with.

He knew better than to doubt his God. The Carcass God had chosen him for this work. The Carcass God had sent the supplies so that the Fra could complete his masterpiece. Surely, all this was not arranged only for the Damned Fra to fail. *He who digs for flesh in the name of the Carcass God will never be called to dig in empty graves.* Miseries, Chapter 9: Verse 1.

The Fra counted bubbles in the water and held his breath. He denied himself breath until the frantic, panicky beat of doubt stilled inside him, and he could once again see the Truth laid out by his God.

The Black Grave had sent him brushes. The Black Grave had sent him paints. The Black Grave needed The Mural to be painted and it would not have called The Damned Fra Anjelico only to watch him fail.

The Fra exhaled.

...All was as it should be.

<u>17</u>

None of this was the way it was supposed to be.

Alex just wanted a night to cut loose. *"Fuck around time is over, son."* That was what his dad had said to him on the night he'd graduated from college... Well, shit on that. Alex missed fuck around time. He was tired of wearing a suit. Tired of 9 AM team meetings and pounding down Tums while he watched millions of dollars in shares rise or fall because some CEO had an opinion about Chik-fil-A.

For just one night, all Alex he wanted to do was get shitty Pennsylvania drunk with his friends. That was it. Instead, here he was. Following a trail of blood through the darkness.

Just make it so we can get him out. Okay, God? I'm not asking for a miracle. I just want us to be able to carry Tommy out of here without the cops or an ambulance getting involved. I'll put my entire next paycheck into the collection plate. I'll throw in my bonus. I'll coach a CYO team. Anything. Please, God. Anything. Anything.

Alex continued in that vein, trailing behind Bridget and Chris, lost in his own head as he offered up any promise (except a vow of celibacy) if this whole mess would somehow resolve itself without any consequences. He barely even heard their muted steps echoing against the stone as they walked. He didn't pick up the different timbre as Bridget and Chris's footsteps fell silent, and it was only Alex still walking through the darkness. He only came back down to earth when he stepped on Bridget's heel and very nearly kept on walking straight over her.

"Shit. Sorry," he muttered.

Bridget didn't answer him. Chris didn't either. The two of them stood side by side in the hallway. The flashlight was aimed at the blood on the floor, but their eyes were fixed on the doorway at the end of the hall.

It was the art classroom. Alex recognized it by the faded construction paper flowers still adorning the door. It looked exactly the way it did ten years ago.

The only difference was the orange light flickering through the glass window in the door. It was not a fluorescent light. It wasn't a flashlight.

Somebody inside that room had started a fire.

Indecision kept them rooted in place. Following the blood had been bad, but having some idea of what was going to happen next had helped keep Chris grounded.

We're going to find Tommy. He's going to be hurt. Maybe we can help him... or maybe we can't. Either way, there's only so many ways this can end.

A firelight looming ahead of them was not supposed to be one of the possibilities. And yet, here it was, casting the row of wooden coat closets in a sickly, halloween glow.

A long, black shadow passed across the light and then disappeared just as quickly. Bridget had already been holding Chris' hand, but she squeezed tighter as an involuntary gasp squeaked from her mouth.

That was too big. That was Chris' immediate reaction. Yes, the shadow had moved so fast that he couldn't get a good look. And yes, shadows always did look bigger than the person casting them.

Still, there was no denying Chris' gut instinct. That shadow was too big to belong to his scrawny cousin Tommy.

None of them moved. They stood, frozen in place, watching the fire dancing from within the room. The same room where the trail of Tommy's blood came to an end.

There was something wrong here. Chris felt the way he always felt during a cage fight, right before the bell was about to ring. Nothing had happened yet, but there was something very dangerous staring back at him, and his whole body was gearing up to deal with it. He looked towards Bridget and she was already staring back at him. Her eyes were wide and unsure behind her glasses. She felt the same unease that Chris did.

Alex finally was the one to push past them. If it was Tommy who'd started the fire, he couldn't be that badly hurt. And if it wasn't Tommy, if some homeless guy had broken in to get out of the storm…. Well, then maybe Alex could call the cops on *him*, and maybe his dad would look past the little detail of what Alex and his friends were doing there in the first place. And if Tommy was really…. *You know,* then maybe nobody had to know that it was Ellen who pushed him in the first place. It wasn't Cutter's fault that Tommy didn't know when to quit. He found himself actually hoping that it was some old drunk shitting on the floor. It would solve a lot of problems.

Thanks, God. That "mysterious ways" shit really pays off.

"Alex!" Chris hissed. Alex swung back towards him and held his hands out, palms up. *What else are we going to do?* He continued to creep towards the door. A moment later, he caught Bridget and Chris creeping along beside him in his peripheral vision. Jesus, they both looked so anxious.

They came to a stop just before the art room door, safely clear from the glass so that nobody inside would be able to see them. Still crouched down, Alex edged towards the corner of the window. *If it's Tommy, we can just put out the fire and get him. If it's somebody else, I'll do the shouting and Chris can be the muscle.* Alex moved forward another inch, enough so that he could see what the orange firelight had to reveal.

…Too much. Oh, Christ. Oh, Jesus. Too much. Too fucking much.

Alex's heart pounded at the back of his throat. The only thing keeping him from a complete meltdown was the fuzzy idea that this was too fucked up to be real. No way this was really happening. No way that they'd gone looking for Tommy Baker and found some fucking man mountain ripping the skin off a human body in the old art classroom.

There was more. A skinless corpse, red and glistening, crumpled in the corner. Oh, Jesus, Alex recognized the tattered rags of Pete's fraternity shirt.

Peterbilt. Ah, Peterbilt.

And the dead body on the table. Alex caught a glimpse of Tommy's face before the giant gave the corpse a hard jerk. Tommy's face rolled away from the door; and the skin on his right arm and torso came away from his flesh like a jacket being shrugged off.

Alex's lower jaw quivered up and down, a burgeoning scream building up like boiling water in a teapot. He was going to scream, he had to, but an ice cold hand clamped over his mouth first. The hand shook with fear, even as it strove to keep Alex's scream pent up.

It was Chris' hand. He'd turned the flashlight off, leaving only the firelight to illuminate his pale, stricken features. He raised a trembling finger to his own lips, urging quiet. He motioned backwards. Back the way they came.

Yes, that was the plan. The... the killer was still ripping away great swaths of Tommy's skin. He hadn't looked through the glass yet. They could go back. They just had to be very... very... quiet.

Chris took the lead with Bridget right behind him. Alex followed as closely as he could without stepping on the redhead's heels. They kept the flashlight off this time, and Alex took great care to make every step as silent as possible. Still, he winced at every echo of his feet in the stone hallway. They hadn't been this loud before, he was sure of it. Why was it so impossible to be silent now?

Ahead of him, Chris and Bridget were holding hands as they made their way down the corridor. Suddenly achingly alone, Alex reached out for Bridget's free hand. His fingers closed around hers- slim, cool, and as restoring as dipping his hand into holy water. He exhaled, reveling in the sensation even as thick, rough fingers enveloped his free hand and cinched it tight in a grip like a bear trap.

Alex shrieked, high and long like a child. He looked over his shoulder. The killer was there. His face hidden by a white shroud spattered with red stains. His dark eyes bored through Alex's soul like a blowtorch through ice. His grip on Alex's hand tightened. Bones creaked and Alex shrieked again. "Chris!"

The two of them turned around just as Alex had his hand ripped away from Bridget's. The maniac let go of Alex's hand and grabbed him by the throat just as quickly. Alex was in the air then, all six feet and hundred and ninety pounds of him hefted as easily as a grocery sack, and slammed hard against the stone wall. Alex's head rocked back and slammed into the wall. His jaw clipped shut, neatly severing the tip of his tongue. Hot salt filled his mouth. Alex screamed, opening his jaws so the blood ran down his chin.

The Fra's dark eyes narrowed as the can sprung a leak, fresh red seeping out to ruin the Lenox Tan. He shifted his grip on the Lenox Tan's throat, forcing the paint's jaw shut. The Fra pulled the hand spike from his sash belt. It was a simple and efficient tool- a wooden handle and six inches of narrow iron tapered to a sharpened point. The Fra raised it high. The Lenox saw it coming. His eyes grew to the size of moons. Blood bubbled against the Fra's palm as the Lenox Tan tried to scream. He raised an arm to ward off the blow.

The Fra easily brought the spike down around the futile attempt to delay The Mural. He didn't even try to aim, trusting the Scapegrace Lochner to guide his strike, and was rewarded with a dull thud running all the way up his shoulder. The frantic bubbling of blood against the Fra's palm slowed and then stopped.

Praise to the Black Grave.

Moving carefully, fearful of any spillage, the Fra set the Lenox down into a sitting position. He surveyed the flesh critically and was satisfied with what he saw. The color was preserved, the blood flow from the cut tongue was already a trickle. The frantic anxiety he'd felt ever since the Chantilly and the fall was already abating. The Carcass God was in control. All was proceeding according to the Will of the Rotted Hand.

The Fra grasped the handle sticking out from the Lenox Tan's skull and yanked the spike out with ease. The sickly thunk echoed in the dark hallway. He stood back up and wiped the iron pick clean on his thigh. No two shades of blood were exactly the same, and even the slightest contamination could not be tolerated.

His head rolled slowly on his shoulders, ball bearings moving in perfect working order. He turned his gaze down the hall to take stock of the other colors.

The Citrine Quartz was still there. He had one hand over the chest of the Vanilla Cream, trying to shield her from the Fra's gaze as they slowly backed away.

Beneath the shroud, the Damned Fra Anjelico grinned. He swung his body towards them. Down the hall, the Vanilla squeaked. The Citrine Quartz put himself more firmly between the Cream and the Fra. "Bridget, run!" he yelled.

Yes, run. Put some more red flush in that skin. Strawberry Cream. The Fra stalked towards them, picking up steam himself. He didn't have all night. Classrooms bustled past him as he closed the distance. His grip tightened around the metal spike.

The Citrine punched out at the Fra's face. Foolishness, the Quartz was still too far out of range, his flicking punch couldn't possibly-

It wasn't a punch. Too late, the Fra saw the dark square coming towards his face.

Chris threw Alex's phone at the faceless gargantuan, and didn't wait to see if it hit him. The distraction was what mattered. Chris lunged, ducked down, and grabbed hold of the killer's thighs to take him down. The psychopath had legs like cement posts, but the leverage was what mattered. Chris twisted, but a hammer fist slammed into his back first and dropped him like a toy with its batteries pulled. Chris sank to his knees, gasping for air.

He tried for the takedown again, but all the strength was gone from his arms. His legs were shot. He couldn't catch his breath. Something hot and wet ran down his shoulder.

Oh, fuck. I think I've been stabbed.

The boot came down on his back next. Chris' arms folded up like empty beer cans. The relentless pressure pinned Chris flat to the ground and held him there. Chris turned his head. His ear was pressed against the icy floor. The sound of his own rushing blood filled his head.

Bridget's scream came even louder. "Get away from him!"

Chris wheezed. That was wrong. He wanted to scream. He desperately needed to scream.

"Bridget, get out of here!" he tried to cry. But his voice was so weak, he barely heard it himself.

Bridget sprinted towards the monster towering over her boyfriend. She had to crane her neck up just to meet the dark eyes lurking behind the blank hood.

No disrespect, ladies, but if you find yourself in an unsafe situation, your attacker is most likely going to be bigger and stronger than you. That was how Chris had began the self-defense class he taught at the gym. Bridget had only taken it as an excuse for him to "correct her form," but she came away with some lessons regardless. *I'm going to teach you some things you can do to get around that and protect yourself, but the first thing you should do, if at all possible, is get yourself a weapon.*

Bridget had her boots, clutching them by the laces in a makeshift flail. She swung for the psychopath's head. The man in the bloody hood stepped back. The heel of Bridget's boot sailed harmlessly past him, but she succeeded in forcing him to step away from Chris. Bridget pushed forward before fear could dissuade her. She swung for the attacker again.

This time, the killer grabbed the swinging boot and yanked it from her with ease. The hand came for her next. The massive paw closed around her throat. Bridget gurgled as she was lifted off her feet and slammed against the wall, just like Alex. The hideous lack of a face was pressed right against her nose. She smelled blood. She felt hot breath seeping through the cloth.

Bridget came up with her other weapon. She had her keys clenched in her fist, the long key to her Ford sticking out from between two knuckles. Bridget punched out and drove the key like a dagger deep into the dark orb of the maniac's eye. She felt only the briefest resistance, and then the key sank into his eye socket. Blood and white jelly ran down the front of his shroud.

The psychopath didn't even flinch. His grip on Bridget's neck only cinched tighter. Black dots began to crowd at the edges of her vision. The killer raised the metal spike high, past the crown of her skull. Bridget let out a muffled scream. She twisted the key in her attacker's eye socket, but the iron pick's mechanical ascent never wavered. It rose high over her head for a death blow.

And then he jerked forward towards her. The full, sickly warm weight of him pressed against her. The bloody cloth of his face mashed against hers. The tip of the spike clattered harmlessly against the block wall.

Wrapped around the killer's waste, Chris twisted hard and brought all three of them crashing down in a kicking tangle on the floor. Chris sprawled his weight over the Fra's back, struggling for control of the spike and throwing elbows at the back of the killer's head.

Pinned at the bottom of the scramble, Bridget was still trapped in the maniac's choking grasp. The massive hand squeezed hard into her flesh, that pressure was the only real sensation Bridget had left. Everything else was going numb as she struggled for air. She groped over the fingers, thick as bottlenecks, remembering Chris' voice even as everything around her became increasingly dim and difficult to remember.

If someone grabs you, you can't get out by just pulling away. And you can't break his grip just by grabbing his hand.

Bridget closed her hands over the hand wrapped around her throat.

"Four fingers. That's like four times the grip, right?"

Bridget grabbed the killer's thumb with both hands. She surged all of her strength behind it, arm muscles bulging.

"The thumb is the weakest part of the grip. You grab his thumb. Just his thumb. You put all your strength on that one weak link and-"

Bridget pried his thumb back like a rusty hinge. She squirmed away and collapsed, sucking in air as color flooded back into her face.

She shook her head. There was no time to recover. She crawled back over to the struggle just as the psychopath got his knees beneath his body and powered back up, squat-thrusting Chris' bulk with ease and tossing him carelessly across the hall with bone-rattling force.

It was Chris that Bridget went to. She grabbed him under the armpits and tried to haul him up. "Hang on, Chris," she muttered. She didn't know if he could hear him. His eyes were unfocused and his breathing was an uneasy rattle. There was a stab wound high on his back near one shoulder. "Come on, sweet cheeks. Get up." That seemed to get through to him. He unsteadily tried to stand and immediately slumped back against the wall. Bridget tried to pull him towards her for support. He was so cold, except for the sickly warm spot where he'd been stabbed.

"Chris. We've got to go," she urged. A shadow fell over them. The psycho in the hood was coming again. There was no time, Bridget pulled Chris harder, but he only sank down to his knees.

"Run," he whispered.

Never. She only pulled harder, raising him to a half crouch.

"Help!" she screamed, hoping Vickie would hear her, but knowing there was no point. He was on them, the massive figure with gore flowing freely from his ruined eye. He was coming. Bridget stopped trying to haul Chris up and simply held him close.

He walked past them. Bridget didn't believe it, even as it happened, but it was true. The shrouded killer strode past, not even acknowledging Bridget as she struggled under Chris' weight.

Instead, he went to Alex's body.

Bridget's car key was still lodged in his eye. He took a moment to dislodge it. The ring of keys played a short, atonal chime as he tossed them aside.

He knelt down, picked up Alex's body, and rose back up, cradling the body with surprising reverence.

Confusion paralyzed Bridget. She thought to try and run, but some perverse instinct warned that might only encourage the psychopath to chase them. She stayed with Chris, frozen in place.

The killer didn't even acknowledge them. He took Alex's body away from them. Back towards the art room and the fires.

Bridget took her chance. "Chris, you have to get up, right now." Breathing fast and shallow, Chris clawed his way to his feet. Bridget pulled his arm over her shoulder coaxed him down the hall. She looked back once, and all she saw was the open door to the art room. Of the killer himself, Bridget saw no sign.

They were halfway down the hall when the voice rang out behind them. It was not a shout. Rather, it was a low, sinewy assurance that whispered off of the stone walls around them.

"See you soon," The Fra called out.

18

The Lenox was exquisite.

The Fra had made the right decision. The longer he spent grappling with the Citrine and the Vanilla Cream, the more the Lenox Tan would have degraded. It wouldn't be like this. The paint he was peeling off of the young body was in perfect condition. The color, the texture…

He had prioritized The Mural, and he had been rewarded for doing so.

The Fra continued working with the black knife. He started at the neck and worked his way up over the chin and around the left cheek. He worked in a semi-circle, taking the whole of the Lenox Tan's face in a long, continuous section.

The Vanilla Cream and the Citrine Quartz still had to be found. So did the Blush Rose and the girl with the lovely White Ochre skin. The Fra would claim them soon. None of them were going anywhere, the storm still howling outside of the school would hold them for now.

The Fra started again on the body's right shoulder and cut outwards to the arm. After the graceless butchery of trying to salvage the Chantilly White, he savored the beautiful ease of preparing the Lenox Tan. The skin was so accommodating. The blood had gushed out so willingly.

The Fra felt no fear as he meticulously continued his preparations. It never occurred to him that his colors might find a way to escape from the school. They were delivered to him by the Carcass God. They were trapped in the palm of the Rotted Hand and held there for the glory of the Fra's work. His God would not do that only to release them again.

The Carcass God let the Chantilly White fall from a balcony. A small voice insisted. *Why didn't It summon a mountain of graveyard dirt to cushion the fall?*

The Fra smothered that voice with ease. He'd scavenged enough of the Chantilly. He had not been denied what he needed.

As he worked, The Fra was careful not to taint the skin with any dribblings from his ruined eye. The loss to his vision did not bother the Fra. As for the pain? He felt nothing at all.

The Faith had made pain a thing of the past for the Fra. The last pain he'd ever felt had been the rope around his neck. And he wasn't even the Damned Fra Anjelico then. He had not been called. He was not yet an Infernal Artist. He had been nothing but paint and meat himself. Thin paint. Weak meat. He'd chosen the rope rather than another day of weakness.

The rope. The pain. And then panic.

Help! He'd tried to wail, even though no words could escape the noose cinched around his neck. He'd kicked. He'd groped fruitlessly at the coarse fibers. *Please! Somebody help me!*

No help came. He'd kicked helplessly, dangling at the end of the rope. Gradually, his body had grown numb. His eyes slipped shut.

And then, in the Darkness, a sensation had rippled across his numb, dying body. Small tingles, starting at his calves and working their way up his body. Slowly, they had multiplied until it felt like his entire body was crawling with skittering, delicate legs.

His sense of smell reawakened next. Curious, considering he could no longer draw breath. Nevertheless, the stench filled his nostrils. It had overpowered even the scent of the shit running down his leg. It was the smell of a dead animal left to rot under a porch, the rotting pelt shoved hard against his nostrils.

He had felt fear at first. The same way the shepherds had first felt fear when the angel appeared in the blasphemy of the nativity story. But the fear faded quickly, replaced by understanding. Something had heard his cry and had reached out to him. The stench of death and the creeping prickle across his skin was a language of its own. He had communed with it. He had understood what it wanted of him.

It wanted service.

It had chosen him. It had selected him for a purpose. Of all the world, this… *power* had selected *him*. It had called *him* to do its bidding.

Yes! He'd sworn. *YES!*

He had opened his eyes, still hanging at the edge of the rope, but the pain was gone. Strength was in his arms as never before. He had pulled himself free from the noose with his bare hands. The first steps he took after touching the ground were the first steps he took on the path to becoming the Damned Fra Anjelico.

No, the Fra did not fear the possibility of losing his color palette. He trusted his God deliver the tools he needed. This was the purpose he had been chosen for. The Carcass God would not abandon him now.

Amen.

19

Officially, 911 operators did not get snow days.

Unofficially, in a very real way, that wasn't true at all.

The first few hours on duty were always rough. Commuters stranded on their way home. Skittish transplants worried their full fridge wouldn't be enough supplies to get through a storm.

But after that, as people got where they needed to be and recognized that the snow wouldn't go on forever, activity slowed to a crawl. People put on Netflix and a blanket and waited for the storm to pass. There was the occasional heart attack or domestic incident, but for the most part, a blizzard was as close to a day at the beach as they were going to get.

There were only two operators on shift. Frank Hayden and Jessica Clark. Jessica was knitting a blanket for her forthcoming grandson, and Frank was sipping on a Coke and reacquainting himself with a biography of John Fitzgerald Kennedy, perhaps the finest man to ever crawl out of that backwoods slum they called New England.

Frank was knee deep the Cuban Missile Crisis. The naval blockade was just about to begin when the ringing of Frank's emergency console called him back to the 21st century. He set his book aside, serious as JFK himself, and answered the call.

"911. What is your emergency?" he intoned.

The response from the other end didn't come at first. The words hitched in the caller's throat, struggling to sob their way out, and Frank knew immediately that this was not a grandfather going into cardiac arrest. This was the stammering, malfunctioning sob of someone whose life had descended into a hell that they'd never thought possible.

"It's alright," he coaxed. "Tell me what the situation is."

"....I... We... Please help us. I'm with my friends at Saint Regina Academy on Sunrise Avenue in Pine Hollow. There's..." the caller's voice broke down into a sob.

Beneath his hardened veneer of neutrality, Frank's hand sought the stress ball on his desk, and clamped down on it hard.

"There's a crazy man in here with us," the girl cried. "He killed Alex. He killed Peter. He stabbed my boy- my boyfr-."

"Where is the attacker now?" Frank interrupted.

There was no answer. Only white noise from the other end of the line. Frank referenced the computer screen for the address and began relaying the incident to emergency services. All the while, he waited for a scream from the other end of the phone. Or the violent soundtrack as the phone was ripped away and the frantic young woman was held down and-

"I don't know where he is. We ran away after he…" the caller couldn't stop herself from sobbing. "Please, we need the police!"

"Listen to me. What's your name?"

"B-b-Bridget."

"Okay, Bridget. The police are coming," Frank assured her. "But the roads are in very bad condition and it's going to take some time. But we're gonna work this out, you and me. Is there anyone with you?"

"My boyfriend's with me. He's hurt. And my best friend Vickie. She's… Oh, God. She doesn't even know he's out there,"

"One thing at a time. Is there any way for you to safely exit the building?"

"I don't know! He's still here. I don't know if he's in the hall or... we're on the second floor now. We tried to open the window, but nobody is supposed to be in the building. There's some kind of lock on the latch to keep it from opening. We could maybe break a window, but…"

She went on, but Frank was only half listening. The stress ball in his hand was condensed to something the size of a peach pit.

"Do you see a secure hiding space anywhere?" the operator asked. He spoke in the same cool, professional tone. Nothing in his smooth inflection revealed his growing certainty that this kid was doomed.

She was right to be afraid of going out into the hallway if the attacker was still on location, especially if she was with somebody injured. Breaking a window did not qualify as a safe exit either . The noise could attract attention and there was a good chance of someone suffering a serious laceration from broken glass.

Especially if they're swan diving out a second-story window.

If they could find a place to hide, they could conceivably stay alive long enough for the police to arrive but, with blizzard conditions outside, emergency services were at least a half hour away. That was a long time to play hide and seek.

"Can you barricade yourself in the room where you're hiding?" he asked. "Blocking the door might be the safest thing for you to do." His voice never wavered, never betrayed a hint of the sweat running down the twelve-year veteran's brow. He heard the boyfriend in the background. Panting. Wincing. *These kids are going to die,* he thought.

"I don't know," Bridget wept. "But the battery on this phone is almost dead. Please. Please send help. We-"

-   -   -

"-Aren't safe here," Bridget pleaded. "He's going to kill us all."

There was no response. The voice on the other end of the phone was gone. Bridget let Chris' phone slip out of her hands.

"It's dead," she told him.

They were hiding inside one of the classrooms, crouched down in the coat closet. Bridget groped for one of Chris' hands in the darkness and squeezed it tight. He went one better and pulled her close against him. Bridget hugged his chest tight, trying to ignore the cold of his front and the terrible warmth of his back. His breathing was awful. It was a strained, rattling wheeze, like an air conditioner struggling to work through a clogged filter.

"But you got through to someone," he said. "They're coming. We just have to keep our heads down until they do. Did he say anything else?"

"He said to barricade ourselves in the room so nobody else can get in. But..." Bridget took a deep breath. "Chris. Vickie's still out there. Ellen too. They have no idea what's happening."

"Oh, shit," he breathed.

"I've got to get them. I can't leave Vickie like that."

His body shifted underneath her.

"I know," he said. "Pick up the phone. At least we can throw it at him if we see him. We just have to move slow and be careful."

"No," Bridget said. She held him in place. "You stay here. I'll find Vickie and Ellen, and I'll bring them back. We'll all wait together."

"And we'll look for them together. I'm not going to sit here in the dark and wait for that fucking lunatic to grab you."

"You can barely move."

He scoffed. "'Tis but a scratch."

She slapped him in the arm before she could remember his condition. "Don't you quote Holy Grail at me, shithead. A month ago you didn't even know what Monty Python was."

His hands found her face and cupped her cheeks. On cue, her eyes adjusted to the dark just enough so she could see his face.

"There's a lot I didn't know a month ago," Chris said. He kissed her and Bridget willingly took refuge in it. For less than a minute, they turned back the clock. They were in a different classroom once again. Bridget was back on the desk, tasting Chris' mouth and feeling his hands against her skin.

Too soon, he had to break the kiss to suck in a wheezing breath, and the memory was over. They were back in the coat closet again. Chris took his hands away from Bridget's face, but he interlocked their fingers instead.

"You're not going anywhere without me, remember? Your words. Not mine."

Bridget kissed him. They were still in the same closet. She tasted blood on his lips.

It was still better than being without him.

<u>20</u>

"There's legal precedent in my favor," Ellen said. It was the first thing either of them had said since Bridget and the others went upstairs.

"DuBeau vs the State of New York," she recited. "Manslaughter charges were dismissed after it was proven that Marissa DuBeau acted in self-defense when she pushed her attacker in front of a subway train. The statute language from state to state is really remarkably similar: 'The use of force upon or toward another person is justifiable when the actor believes that such force is immediately necessary for the purpose of protecting oneself against the use of unlawful force by such other person on the present occasion.'"

The nurse's office was the room closest to the stairwell. Ellen and Vickie had retreated there, with the door propped open so they would be able to hear anybody coming back down. The old cot with cracked vinyl was still there. Vickie got Ellen to lie down and then pulled a chair over so she could sit close by the blonde's head. Ellen had laid there with her hands folded over her stomach, completely still, for longer than Vickie felt comfortable.

"And I didn't even act with malicious intent," Ellen went on. "I didn't mean for him to fall like that. I was just trying to get him off me. All I did was push him to the side. If he hadn't lost his balance, maybe he wouldn't have…"

"I think the important thing is that you didn't cause any of this, Ellen. He was the one that followed you," Vickie said. "He tried to rape you."

"It's not that simple," Ellen said. "Somebody's going to say that I led him on. His family's not going to accept that he did anything wrong. They're going to look for some way to blame me. But the law works in my favor," she stressed, as if Vickie had disagreed with her. "And if Tommy really isn't… I mean, if they find him and he's really not… I don't want trouble," Ellen said. "I just want to get on with my life."

"You will," Vickie said. "This little asshole isn't going to keep you from doing anything. You're gonna get the fuck out of this town and pass the bar and fight for the legal right to have a gun and a portrait of Jesus in every classroom in America."

Vickie saw the ghost of a smile in the dim light. "Thank you for staying with me, Vickie," Ellen said.

Vickie had been very careful not to initiate contact between them, but she reached out and squeezed Ellen's hand. She would have let it go just as quickly, but Ellen grabbed on with her other hand and kept Vickie's hand cradled in her grasp.

From outside, they heard the echoing yawn of a door opening. Ellen's grip tightened and the fear that had dulled in her eyes flared to life again. She squeaked.

"I'll see what's going on," Vickie assured her. "Just stay here."

Vickie was almost out the door when the faint tremor of Ellen's voice reached out for her. "Vickie?" she asked.

Vickie looked back over her shoulder. "Yeah?"

Ellen sat up. Here in the nurse's office, the snow was almost up past the windows, but muffled orange light from the street filtered into the room, dressing her in a tangerine glow. "...Will you kiss me?"

Vickie nodded. She came back and knelt down in front of her. The kiss was scarcely more than chaste, but it lingered and hit both of them like a much needed sip from a warm drink.

"I'll be back," Vickie said. "Okay?"

Ellen nodded.

Vickie stepped into the hall. Her night vision was completely shot in the windowless hallway, but she turned in the direction of the stairwell, one hand trailing against the wall so she didn't get lost.

"Bridget!" she called out. "Are you guys there? Did you find Tommy?"

Nobody called out in return, but she heard someone coming down the stairs. Slow, plodding steps.

"Bridget, what's going on? Pete, if that's you, no more pranks. There's a lot of bad shit going on."

Vickie was close enough now that she could make out the looming shape of the stairs. And still, no answer. But someone was there. Maybe Tommy had somehow slipped past the others? The visual came to her fully formed, a perverse twist on the inspiration that led to most of her best work.

Tommy plodding down the steps like a zombie. His skull cracked open. Gaping mouth full of broken teeth. Disengaged eyes staring at something a thousand miles away. Blood gushing down his front. Splashing down the steps. Dark reds. Chalk white. Scratchy colored pencils.

The thought of it sent shivers down Vickie's spine. She closed her eyes and tried to erase the image from her mind. *Shit. Please, anything but that.*

Vickie came to the bottom of the steps. She peered up just as a massive, shambling shape came out of the blackness. It reached towards her and Vickie screamed. She staggered back. "No! Stay away!"

"Vickie, it's me!" Bridget hissed.

The shape split in two. Half of the thing leaned against the railing and the other half, significantly smaller, came towards her.

Not one shape, Vickie realized now. It was Bridget and Chris. They'd been clinging to each other, but Chris was now doubled over the bannister while Bridget ran down the final steps and enveloped Vickie in a constricting embrace.

"We have to be quiet," Bridget whispered. "He could be anywhere. I don't think he followed us. We didn't hear anything. But I don't know." Her shoulders shook. Vickie felt the wetness of tears against her neck, and a different wetness where Bridget clutched at her back. Hotter. Stickier.

Oh my God. Is that blood?

"We have to get out of here, Vickie. Right now. Where's Ellen?"

"She's in the nurse's office," Vickie whispered, mimicking Bridget's hushed tone. She didn't know what was going on, and she didn't waste time asking. If Bridget was afraid, she had good reason. If she said run, Vickie would run. "I don't know where Pete-"

"Pete's dead. Pete's dead too. Get Ellen. We're leaving."

"Vickie?" Ellen called out. She came hesitantly up the hallway. "Vickie, what's happening!?" she made no effort to lower her voice.

"Ellen, you have to be quiet!" Chris whispered, raising his voice as much as he dared.

Vickie scrambled back towards Ellen, trying to move as silently as she could. Bridget's terror was contagious.

"Pete's dead too." ...Who else is dead? Why isn't Alex with them?

Time for that later. Vickie was close enough now to pick Ellen out of the gloom. She stood a little taller. Vickie could see that her posture was more defined. Some of the shellshock had cleared her personage. Vickie patted the air, trying to signal for Ellen to be quiet, but Vickie could see that Ellen didn't understand what she was trying to do.

And Vickie could see the massive figure that materialized from the darkness behind Ellen. A massive, hulking figure without a face.

"Ellen, look out!" Vickie screamed.

It was too late. The hand clamped down on Ellen's shoulder before Vickie could even finish her warning. A second massive hand closed around her jaw. Vickie was even closer now. Close enough to make out just a hint of Ellen's wide, confused eyes before that giant hand whipped back, like someone trying to start a lawn mower, and shattered Ellen's neck. Her vertebrate exploded with a sound like breaking Christmas ornaments. Her head twisted all the way around. Vickie wasn't looking at Ellen's eyes anymore- she was looking at the back of Ellen's head.

Ellen's legs dropped out from under her, but she didn't collapse. The same hands that had murdered her caught Ellen's body and deposited it gently on the floor.

Then, the shadow stood and stepped over the corpse.

Heading straight for Vickie.

She screamed and hastily backpedaled, she couldn't dare turn to take her eyes off him. He seemed to fill up the entire hallway. This tremendous thing coming down on her like a landslide. He reached behind his back and produced a giant iron spike, almost like a magic trick.

"Vickie, run!" Bridget screamed.

It snapped her out of it. Vickie turned.

And slipped in the pool of Tommy's blood.

She didn't go down completely. She pinwheeled her arms and fought for balance. She slipped to one knee but managed to keep from falling on her ass.

It all took just enough time for the murderer to catch up to her. He raised the spike and Vickie's entire body went cold. Everything slowed down. She was aware of the heavy, booming breath of the man with the spike. She smelled the blood she was crouching in. She was aware of the flexing muscle as the spike came down on her head.

She heard the growing roar as Bridget sprinted past her and leapt in front of the spike.

"NO!" she yelled.

The Fra delayed his killing blow as the Vanilla Cream leapt into his path. The angle was wrong now. The spike through the White Ochre's skull would gouge the Cream's face. Completely unacceptable. He twisted instead, moving the spike aside and bringing around his free arm to palm the Vanilla Cream's head. He caught her skull like a basketball and swung her towards the wall, but there was more momentum behind it then he anticipated. Her head struck concrete and produced a cracking sound like a breaking walnut.

The Damned Fra pulled her back, the Ochre on the floor completely forgotten. The Vanilla Cream lay his grasp, dazed but alive. And not bleeding, Carcass God be praised. Her skin was unbroken. In fact... No, it was too dark in the hallway. He couldn't be sure.

But if he was right...

The Ochre lunged at him. Little more than an afterthought, the Fra met her with his clenched fist. He punched her just beneath the diaphragm. The White Ochre doubled over and sank to her knees, mouth moving soundlessly as she sucked for air.

The Citrine Quartz lurched down the stairs. "Get away from her!" he wheezed.

The Fra felt brief admiration that the color was still standing. The Fra had punctured his lung during their fight. Minimal bleeding, but it should have crippled him completely. He should have been curled up in one of the classrooms, struggling just to breathe. Yet, here he was, gamely pushing forward one step at a time. Trying to defy the Damned Fra Anjelico and his claim to the paints.

It was going to be an honor to boil him down to the purity of his color.

But to all things their time. The Vanilla Cream stirred weakly in his grasp, rising from her daze.

Somewhere, far outside the sealed chamber where Vickie fought to breathe, she sensed the killer pulling away.

With Bridget!

Vickie fought to get back up, but... the punch. She'd never taken a physical blow like that before. She couldn't hear. Her limbs were vapor locked. Her entire body was hitching. Fighting just to unfurl from the fetal position on the floor took everything she had.

Vickie sucked in a breath. Then another. She surged up to her feet and staggered in a light-headed daze. She forced herself to keep pulling in air, replenishing her body.

But why was she even breathing? How could she stagger around like this with that maniac still-

Her head finally cleared. The psychopath was gone. Ellen's body was no longer crumpled in the hallway.

Bridget was gone too.

Only Chris was there. Staggering down the hall with blood running from his back, dribbling down his leg and onto the floor.

Vickie followed after him, wobbling on the legs of a newborn deer.

"Chris!" she shouted.

He ignored her. He took one slow, dragging step forward. And then another.

"Chris, stop!" Vickie caught up with him and grabbed his arm. She was on the verge of tears. Terror and fear ached at the edges of her face. She forced him to look at her.

"Did he... Did he kill Bridget?" she asked.

He shook his head. His own eyes were tormented. He looked like Vickie felt.

"He took her upstairs," Chris said. "I know where. We have to-"

He swayed on his feet and nearly fell over. Vickie caught him first. She threw his arm over her shoulders and pushed them forward. Together.

"Tell me where we're going," she said.

"The art room," Chris wheezed. "He's taking her to the art room."

<u>21</u>

The Fra saw immediately that he'd made the right decision. There was no real way of knowing in the darkness of the hallway. But here, in the firelight, there was no mistaking it.

He'd made it back to his studio at a run. He'd carried the bucket of Blush Rose over his shoulder and he had the dazed, whimpering Vanilla cradled under his arm. Now, he shouldered the Blush Rose's body onto a table. Both hands freed, he carried the Vanilla Cream closer to the light.

Bridget whimpered and tried not to scream as the killer carried her further into the art room. His shrouded face betrayed nothing. The single eye staring out from the bloodstained hood crawled over her like a spider.

I won't scream. I won't scream.

She came to the row of bubbling pots. Each one filled to brimming with bubbling, viscous liquid that smelled like bacon.

The skin. That's the skin. That's what he does with the-

Bridget shuddered in his grasp. She fought the urge to be sick.

"We called the police," she said. "They're on their way here."

I hope so, the Fra thought. *Art's meant to be appreciated.*

But how she looked was far more important than what she had to say. The bruising was already coming up, darkening the Vanilla Cream with swirls of Blueberry and Raven's Feathers.

So much skin bruised poorly, he reflected. Most people turned ugly shades of Wet Gravel and Gunpowder when they were hurt.

But not this skin.

The Fra moved in a burst of violence. He slammed her down on the table. He lifted her high and hammered her back down as hard as he could.

The Cream screamed.

Yes. Good!

The Fra slammed her down again, holding her by the legs and shoulders so he could smash her back flat against the hard surface of the table. Let her entire back open up like mottled butterfly wings!

Her face next. He pinned the Vanilla Cream down by her neck. He clenched his hand into a tremendous fist and leaned in close to her. He breathed deep of her terror.

"I'm going to make such colors out of you," he whispered.

The door behind him flew open before the Fra could beat another streak of blue and black into the Vanilla Cream. He whirled around, already knowing what he was going to find.

The Fra was not disappointed. The White Ochre and the Citrine Quartz had come. They huddled shoulder to shoulder. Their colors faded by blood loss and fear.

But beautiful. Still oh so beautiful.

And they had come to him. They had not hidden themselves away and made him dig them out. They had offered themselves up to him, the final colors before the Mural could begin.

Praise to the Black Grave.

Vickie stood next to Chris. His whole body gave off heat in feverish waves now. He was trembling beside her, and Vickie had no way of knowing if it was sheer terror or his body going into seizures.

For herself, it was fear. Rushing through the door had been unthinking. There was no time to be afraid. There was only the need to find Bridget.

There was time to be afraid now. The room was a slaughterhouse. Red stains glistened on every table. Three skinless bodies lay piled in the corner. Ellen's body lay only a few feet away. Her chest lay flat against the table, but her twisted head stared up at the ceiling.

Todd… oh fucking God…. Todd!?

And in the center of it all, swelling to fill the entire room… *him.*

The killer made no move towards them. He casually drew the long spike from his waist. He stared at them through that filthy rag, one eye a ruin of gore, and there was such *joy* blazing in his remaining eye. That bliss looked more dangerous to Vickie than the spike. It pinned her in place.

Chris pushed her into action. "Get Bridget and get her out of here!" Chris lifted his fists, chest heaving like each breath weighed fifty pounds, and shuffled towards the monster in the hood.

The Citrine Quartz came forward, wheezing like a typhoid victim. Offering himself up to be the next color added to his palette.

At least, he thought he was offering himself. The truth was that the Rotted Hand of the Carcass God had chosen him. It was the Will of He Who Rots in the Earth that guided all things.

Then let it be so. The Fra raised the spike.

Chris pushed himself forward, trying to ignore the weakness in his limbs and the pain in his back that felt like a nest full of stinging wasps. *You're trained. You can do this.*

Bullshit he was. There was no training for this. He didn't want to die.

But, in the corner of his eye, he saw that Vickie had reached Bridget. She was helping her off the table. Pulling her away towards the hall. Away from the killing room.

Chris exhaled. His heartbeat didn't slow down, but at least it steadied. He didn't want to die. He wanted to live in a basement apartment with Bridge and keep their change in a coffee can so they could eventually afford to go out to dinner. But if all of that wasn't in the cards... Vickie was getting Bridget out. That was the only thing that mattered.

He swayed at the waist and stared down the maniac with the metal spike. The pain and weariness didn't leave his body, but they faded. Chris put them on a high shelf at the back of his mind, far from where he needed to worry about them. *Okay... okay...*

The Fra charged, unleashed like a rockslide. He brought the spike down in a stabbing arc. Chris twitched at the waist. The iron point missed his shoulder by centimeters. He felt it tug at the fabric of his sweater.

But Chris had felt a thousand punches miss by the same kiss of air, and he knew what to do in return. His right hand came up in an automatic reaction, came up in an uppercut with all of his bodyweight driving behind it. Even before the punch connected, Chris knew it was a devastator. Juan Manuel Marquez countering Manny Pacquiao into oblivion. Conor McGregor destroying Jose Aldo with one punch. The punch lifted off with the force of a Saturn V rocker and smashed flush underneath the maniac's jaw. The impact cracked two of Chris' own knuckles, but he felt the psycho's jaw break apart like a pinata. A smattering of broken teeth rattled out from behind the filthy cloth shroud.

The Damned Fra Anjelico reacted with the same automatic ease. He gripped Chris' wrist before the teeth had finished falling and held on tight.

Chris knew what to do. *Snap your arm back hard. Flex against the thumb and break his grip*. But reality moved too fast. The Damned Fra surged forward, bulldozing Chris ahead of him. Chris tried to plant his feet. He threw one leg back to give himself a wider base of support. He fired off short punches with his free hand and lashed out with a headbutt that made his own eardrums ring.

None it even slowed down the relentless force of the Damned Fra Anjelico. He forced the Citrine's arm against the closet door, pinning it in place. The spike followed a second later. The Fra stabbed through the Quartz's wrist and into the closet door behind it.

The paint screamed. His legs collapsed out from under him but the spike held firm, stringing him up by his skewered wrist. The Quartz kept screaming. Some mad reflex made him tap out with his free hand while his legs skittered uselessly beneath him and all of his body weight bore down on the iron stake jammed deep into the door. The Citrine Quartz howled. Drool ran from his gaping mouth.

The Damned Fra grabbed the Quartz by the chin and forced his jaw shut. He slammed the Citrine's head against the closet door. Not even hard enough to bruise. Enough to hold him still while the Fra attended to-

"Chris!" the Vanilla Cream screamed.

Ah. Thank you, My God.

Vickie almost had Bridget to the door. They were right at the threshold when Bridget looked over her shoulder, just in time to see Chris manhandled into the closet and the spike pierce his wrist.

"Chris!" she yelled.

"NO!" Vickie tried to stop her, but it was too late. Bridget pulled herself free.

Kind Bridget.

Loving Bridget.

Unfailingly dedicated, unquestionably loyal Bridget.

Smart Bridget. Too smart just to throw herself at her boyfriend's attacker. She went to the table instead, where the iron cauldrons bubbled and hissed. Bridget lifted one of the vats off its brazier. The contents sloshed and sizzled. The maniac's eye radiated fear for the first time. He lunged towards Bridget, but the violent authority was gone from his body language. All Vickie sensed in him now was panic.

The killer reached Bridget just as she reared back and flung the boiling contents in his face.

The Fra screamed as molten flesh soaked the shroud and scalded his skin. To an onlooker, his screams were cries of pain, but it was not his body he cried for. It was not his sight that he howled for, even as boiling skin gushed over his clenched eyelid and sealed it shut.

My paints!

He'd had a glimpse of the color just before darkness clamped over him. It was the Chantilly she'd thrown at him. And he had so little to spare.

My paints! My paints!

He groped blindly through the air. *Where is she!?* His thigh struck the table. The Fra whirled in the other direction, hooked fingers swinging through the darkness and snaring nothing.

I'll find her. I'll rip her to fucking pieces.

The Fra stomped. He roared. He banged into tables. All the while, the Citrine screeched and slammed against the closet door.

And, underneath it all, scarcely louder than two snowflakes crashing together... the Vanilla Cream whimpered. The Damned Fra keyed onto the sound. He stuck his hands into the darkness and reached for the sound, trusting the Scapegrace Lochner to guide his grasp.

He was rewarded by the sensation of Cream's trachea trembling in his grasp. The Fra seized on the feeling and tightened his grip.

Yes!

The Fra forced his eye open. Boiling flesh had sealed it closed, and the effort nearly tore his eyelid off, but it was worth it to see the Vanilla Cream turning Nimbus Grey in his hands. He had her! She beat at his hand, but no tricks this time. He slammed her down on his supply table, knocking his brushes and pallet mixers to the floor in an ugly pile.

The Fra didn't care. He didn't care about the mess, or the molten skin fusing his shroud to his face. He only cared about the wasted Chantilly burned into his arms. And this self-righteous heretic who had dared to touch his paints.

Chris watched Bridget thrash helplessly. "Get away from her!" he screamed. He'd already screamed so much. His throat was scoured with rock salt.

Bridget stared at him from the table. She croaked, but no words could escape the massive, scalded hand pressing down on her throat.

But her eyes... Jesus, her eyes. She was so terrified.

Chris lunged up with his free hand and grasped the spike sticking out of his wrist. He gritted his teeth and strained with all his might to pull his arm loose. The spike, wedged firm in the wood, didn't so much as wiggle.

You have to get it out. Bridget's going to die if you don't. Chris took everything he felt for Bridget Tersea Fallon- all of his love. All of his fear. And he put it behind one last titanic effort to pull himself free. He pulled at the spike until the ligaments in his shoulder strained and then tore.

...It wasn't enough.

The Fra took up the skinning knife from the table. He turned the black blade in his hand and held it like a common murder weapon. The Fra did not see the obsidian knife. He did not see the Cream's red hair splayed on the table, or the blue ocean in her wide, horrified eyes as he raised the knife high above her. All he saw was the Chantilly White. Thrown away. Wasted.

"Hey!" a voice screamed at him. The Fra ignored it. He took the black knife and he stabbed it deep into the Vanilla Cream's gut. Her whole body writhed beneath his wrath. The Fra felt the vibrations, channeled through the knife in her flesh and transmitted up his arm and into his soul. It quenched his vengeance some, but he had so much more hatred to leach out. He yanked the knife out of her flesh and raised it again.

The maniac plunged his knife into Bridget's stomach, and Vickie howled like the last coyote on earth. Everything, every horror that she'd witnessed, Vickie would have gladly lived through it a dozen times over rather than see her best friend pinned on a table with a knife through her stomach. Blood turning her shirt red. More blood seeping from her mouth as she gurgled out a moan.

The killer in the filthy hood yanked the knife out of Bridget's stomach and raised it above his head once more.

Vickie screamed again. This time, there was a prehistoric excuse for a word buried inside her wretched shriek. The same word Vickie had screamed at him in a final, desperate attempt to distract him from her best friend.

"Hey!"

Vickie didn't wait for his reaction this time. She lashed out and knocked another one of the boiling vats off its brazier. Dark brown molasses washed over the floor. The heavy iron pot followed shortly after.

The Fra looked up before the sound of the pot fell. It was the splashing that got his attention first. Only one thing in that room could make a sound like that. He saw the Alcazar Brown spreading in a growing pool on the floor. The Ochre stood beside the spilled pot. She actually dared to look him in the eye, her mouth twisted in a defiant snarl, before racing out of his studio.

The Damned Fra Anjelico chased after her, mindless as a dog chasing after a rabbit. He left the Vanilla Cream and the Citrine Quartz to bleed and spoil. The only thing he took with him was the bloody knife.

Punish. Punish. Punish.

That was the closest thing to a thought inside his head. She was going to pay. The White Ochre was going to pay dearly for touching his paints.

The Fra burst into the hallway and swung his remaining eye wildly from side to side. She was already gone. A frustrated growl seeped from behind his ruined shroud.

But it didn't matter. The Fra could find her.

All he had to do was follow the trail.

The trail of beautiful, squandered Alcazar Brown footprints stamped on the stone floor.

The Damned Fra Anjelico set off after the footprints.

22

It was just one time.

That was the bleak, desperate comfort Vickie clung to. Bridget, her best friend, had only been stabbed through the torso one time.

People can survive that. Inigo Montoya did it. Stomach wounds don't kill you right away. She just needs to get to a hospital. Chris said they got through to 911. Help's on the way. In the meantime, she needs pressure on the wound. Gotta get back upstairs and stop the bleeding.

But first, the lunatic with the knife needed to be stopped.

Vickie crouched barefoot underneath a table in the cafeteria. She tried to ignore the pounding of her heart. She tried to control her breathing and ignore the biting cold gnawing at her bare feet. She wished that she could have kept her socks on at least, but the polished floor was too slippery to chance it.

You're not going to slip, she told herself. *You're not going to lose your balance, or drop the bottle, or lose your nerve at the last second. You're going to end this and you're going to save Bridget. You're even going to save Chris. You're all getting out here.*

As she ran from the classroom, Vickie was aware of the trail of liquid marking her every step. Her first instinct was to throw her shoes away right then, but a deeper instinct urged her to wait.

Hiding in the shadows, Vickie waited for the killer to come.

Stay calm.

The trail of her footprints led back to the kitchen.

Deep Breaths. But not too loud.

Vickie's shoes and socks were stuffed in one of the ovens, but Vickie herself was hiding on the far opposite side of the cafeteria.

In.... Out... In... Out

She'd turned off all the lanterns, placing herself deeper in the dark. She had a heavy, empty bottle of tequila clutched in her hands. She waited to hear the cafeteria door open. She waited to see the killer's shadowy bulk gliding across the cafeteria. And the longer she waited, the closer her shaky sense of calm came to shattering. She closed her eyes and repeated the "plan" to herself over and over again.

Break the bottle over his head and then shove it in his face. Slash his throat. Slash his face. Don't stop until he stops moving.

Break the bottle over his head and then shove it in his face. Slash his throat. Slash his face. Don't stop until he stops moving.

Break the bottle over his head and then shove it in his face. Slash his throat. Slash his face. Don't stop until he stops moving.

Don't stop.

Don't stop.

Powerful, meaty hands seized her by the legs and dragged her out from under the table. The shadowy hulk pulled her up. Vickie screamed and swung the bottle at the dark moon of her attacker's head.

He snatched it from her hand and flung it away, turning the bottle into a million useless shards of glass.

"Where is he?"

The same hand that had thrown the bottle came back around and slapped her hard across the face.

"Where's my son?" the shadow demanded.

The drunk bitch gawked at him with confused, bleary eyes. She was so fucked up on booze and God knew what else, she probably didn't even know her own name. Mark Fogarty resisted the urge to hit her again.

"Darling," he said placidly, "There's a big bag of rock salt in the Range Rover that I nearly totaled on my way here. Now, every single trespasser in this building is gonna get a double helping of that salt shoved right up their ass. But you've got a unique opportunity here. If you tell me where I can find my shit-eating, bastard little boy, maybe I'll let you slide. So it's up to you. Do you want to tell me where my son is? Or do I go back to my trunk?"

A person, Vickie realized. *Oh, God.* Vickie thought. *Oh, thank you, God.* Vickie clung to the man's coats. The slap was already forgotten. Here was someone from Outside. Here was light and sanity and, most of all, *help.* "We have to leave. We have to get out of- No! Bridget! We have to get Bridget," she babbled. "And Chris. They're-"

The man struck her in the stomach. It was like hitting a mute button. Vickie dropped to her knees, gasping for air. She didn't have the breath to speak, but her lips still moved ceaselessly, desperately trying to form the words she needed to say.

We have to save Bridget. You have to help us.

While he waited for his new friend to decide if she wanted to talk sense, Mark switched on his maglite and swept the powerful beam of light across the cafeteria. "Isn't this a goddamn sight," he muttered. Mark had come in through the front entrance, powering his Land Rover almost all the way up to the doors. His walk down the hall had been incident free, and he'd begun to hope that maybe his son wasn't here after all. Maybe, just *maybe,* he'd miscounted his keys.

But no, the cafeteria was always the most likely place for trouble, and here it was. He swept his light across scattered beer cans and pizza boxes. The whole cafeteria reeked of spilled liquor. And was that a goddamn heater in the corner? Why not just take a fucking blowtorch to the building?

And this is just the start I'm sure. I'm going to make them lick this place clean with their fucking tongues.

"Wait," Vickie pleaded. Still on the floor. She pushed hair back and tried to catch her breath. "You don't….."

"Stand up," Mark snarled. "You've been on your knees enough for one night. Stand up and show a little goddamn maturity."

"Listen to me," Vickie sobbed. "You have to listen. He's been killing us. Oh God. Oh God."

Mark's lip curled. He kicked Vickie hard in the ass. "I said get up, cunt."

The girl didn't stand. The girl actually crawled away from him like a baby, blubbering all the while. It made Mark want to puke, even if it did offer him an uninhibited view of her meaty ass. Mark reached out. He was entitled to a little feel for all the shit he'd gone through. And if the little skank complained, who would believe her?

Something *snapped* behind him. Dry and sharp. Mark whirled around and shined his light at the far side of the cafeteria.

"Who's there!?" he bellowed. "Whatever you just broke, for your sake it better be cheap because the price is coming out of your ass!"

No response. Of course not. None of them had the backbone to answer for anything.

A hand pulled at his leg. The girl was back. "It's *him*," she whispered in a shaky tremor. For a brief moment, the space of a single breath, her sheer, naked terror pierced the cloud of rage that separated Mark from his senses. He replayed in his head what she'd said to him when he first found her.

Killing? Did she say killing?

But the mess.

And the heater.

And that snap. That fucking snap.

"Alex, you are past my last nerve," he roared. "I want you to come out this FUCKING instant!"

The response came flying from the darkness just outside of the flashlight's glare. Came flying like a witch's broom from a halloween decoration- a long, slim shaft with a fat bundle of fiber threads trailing from the tail end. The spear struck Mark in the throat and left him rigid, trembling, and, for the first time since he arrived, silent.

It was a mop, not a broomstick. Vickie saw that with all too much clarity. She saw the jagged edge of the broken mop handle protruding from the back of Mark Fogarty's neck. He spun slightly, and now she saw the dreadlocked mop head. The handle had gone so far through Mark's neck, the tendrils of long white fabric were pressed all the way under his chin, hanging down in a grotesque parody of a Dumbledore beard.

Then Mark hiccupped and a gout of blood burbled from his mouth, staining his beard black in the dim light.

Mark twitched violently. He slid to the left- gurgling and dribbling out more blood. The flashlight slipped from his strengthless fingers and rolled across the floor, casting a roving searchlight across the far wall as it tumbled across the floor.

Then, as if he were the lucky member of a studio audience, the beam slowed and then settled to a stop directly on the hulking figure of the killer with the shrouded face.

Vickie shrieked. She crawled faster, scrambling for dubious shelter underneath a table.

He grabbed her first. He yanked Vickie back and flipped her over. He dropped the brute weight of his body down onto her torso. His industrial vice of a hand squeezed around her throat. The maniac stuck his face right in front of hers. Oh, Christ, she saw every stain. Every oozing fluid from his ruined eye. Worst of all, she saw the mad triumph in his remaining eye.

He had her. And he knew it.

Vickie wheezed out another scream. *Help,* she mouthed, but there wasn't even a whisper of a sound. He lifted the knife. The blade still wet with Bridget's blood. He brought it to Vickie's face, tracing the contour of her cheek. The knife was cold. Sticky.

"You're going to be my sky," he whispered.

His hand tightened around Vickie's throat. He raised the knife high.

The Ochre reached up towards him, futilely trying to stop his blade. Feeble thing. Pathetic shade. The Fra brought the knife down at the same time he realized that it wasn't the knife her fumbling hands sought. Vickie grasped at the rag over his face and yanked it askew, dragging the fabric over the Fra's remaining eye and plunging him into darkness.

The Damned Fra stabbed down anyway. He couldn't see, but that didn't matter. He trusted the Rotted Hand to guide his blade down into the lush valley of her chest. *It is not my hand that swings the blade, Lord,* he prayed. *Not my hand and not my sight. It is yours.*

And the Fra's reward was good. He couldn't see the knife punch through her body, but he felt the thrumming in his bones. He felt the quivering resistance of the Ochre's flesh, and plunged his blade deeper still until it punched through bone. The satisfying vibrations ran up his arm and sent chills down his spine. He heard the Ochre gasp her last breath. Elation soared through him. They were all his now. His pallet was complete. He heaved a satisfied sigh.

A sigh that turned into a moan as searing pain bit down in his hand. It raced up his arm and nestled like coiled fire at the base of his skull. The fire caught and burned wild through his head. The Fra screamed. Somewhere beneath his agony, he felt the Ochre squirm free from his grasp.

What was it? Gods, what was happening to him? The Fra let go of the knife. He groped for his shroud and clumsily straightened it, restoring his sight and revealing what had gone so terribly wrong.

The knife had indeed struck flesh. The Fra had stabbed himself in the hand.... And it *hurt*. The Fra rolled onto his back and clutched his wrist. The knife had gone all the way through his hand. The tip of the blade poked out of his palm like a piece of seashell sticking out of the sand. His breath boomed hot and damp underneath the rag. Far away, the Fra heard someone whimpering.

It took a long moment for him to realize that the pitiful mewling came from his own lips.

Vickie finally found her feet and staggered away, clutching her bleeding throat. Blood seeped from between her fingers and dribbled onto the floor. Searing, intense pain flared from a spot on her throat the size of a dime. The Damned Fra's thrust had been blunted by the meat and bone of his own hand, and the thick cartilage in Vickie's trachea had kept the knife from doing anything more than breaking through her skin.

That's what a doctor would have told her. At the moment, all Vickie really knew was that she was still alive, and she had to keep running if she wanted to stay that way.

Abandoned behind her, a man named Colin Epstein writhed on his back in mortal agony. He moaned like a woman in labor. He still wore the rag, but Colin Epstein was the

Damned Fra Anjelico no longer. The Fra had faith. The Fra knew no pain. The Fra could do all things through his belief in the Communion of Carrion.

Colin Epstein had a knife stuck in his hand. And a broken jaw. And one of his eyes was fucking *gone.* Everything hurt. His whole body sang of suffering and misery.

Why? Why had the Carcass God misguided his hand? Why had he been left to feel this pain?

"Tahm!" he cried out. "Ab-Dan Debahr Gramig!" He cried out in the dead language of the Corpse God: *"Lord! Darken the Path of Your Servant!"*

The Lord did not answer. The prayer died on Colin's tongue, lost in another garbled howl. He tried to meditate on the tale of the Despairing Sitkamose, he who recanted his faith during the Inquisition and had his eyes gouged out by ravens.

Or was that Walter in the Tower of London? There was too much pain. Too much doubt. It made everything hazy and far away.

Carmine.

The word sliced through everything. It was not a person. Not a heretic. It was the color soaking both of his hands. The dark red, with just a hint of purple, pumping from his wounds. Colin sat up. He grasped the knife handle sticking out of his hand. The pain flared. It made Colin want to gasp, but he fought back the urge. He focused on the beautiful red pooling in his palm.

Colin tightened his grip on the knife. More beautiful carmine flowed from his flesh, rich and thick like molten candle wax. Colin yanked the blade loose and tossed it aside. He found his feet. He wandered away from the pool of blood he'd wallowed in and settled beside a relatively clear patch of floor.

Colin clenched his fist. The throbbing in his gored hand doubled, but Colin only squeezed tighter. An act of pure will. The blood flowed thicker from his hand, and Colin dribbled it across the floor in a winding, lazy, "S" pattern. He finished the design and then he traced it again, going back the other way. And then he retraced it again. And again. The winding path grew slightly thicker each time Colin went over it, repeating the scarlet line again and again with perfect precision until it was as plump as a fattened cobra. His hand wanted to tremble, but Colin held it steady. He did not waver.

When the red path was set, Colin moved to the side and created a separate pool of blood. He waited patiently until he'd formed a Carmine puddle the size of a dinner plate. Colin dipped his fingers into the blood and etched small, triangular shapes along the length of the curving red "S." His blunt fingers lacked the finesses for fine detailing, leaving his work with a blurred, impressionist effect, but the final result was unmistakable.

He'd drawn red ships sailing along a river of blood.

And at the base of the river, the destination of the ships, Colin sketched a drop-off, a waterfall, and added a circle of jagged points at the bottom. Whether they were meant to be teeth or rocks didn't matter. What mattered was they formed a ring. And, in the center of the ring, Colin smeared a mass of questing tentacles rising up to claim the boats. The coils of Niojsu, the Entrapper.

Colin made a few finishing touches. By this point, his hand no longer ached and the smeared haze in the right side of his vision felt as natural as if he'd lived with it for his entire life. He gazed upon his finished work, savoring the perfection of what he'd wrought.

For your glory, my God.

Restored, the Damned Fra Anjelico rose back up.

23

He did not see the girl. The White Ochre. For a moment, panic seized him. Agony once again gnawed at the Fra's ruined hand and eye.

And then the Fra focused on the blood. Little spit-spots of Merlot Red on the floor, starting at his feet and leading down the hall. The pain disappeared as quickly as it had resurfaced. Praise be to the Black Grave.

The Damned Fra followed the blood. No trickery now, not like with the Alcazar Brown. The red could only be coming from one source. It led from the cafeteria into the total darkness of the of the hallway, but that didn't matter. The one-eyed artist picked out the bloody splotches with ease. Hazy sunsets against a pitch black canvas.

The Fra dragged his blade against the stone wall, reveling in the atonal scream as he followed the trail. He hoped the Ochre could hear it. The extra dread pumping in her blood would do wonders for the paint.

The trail didn't go far. It led to a door right there in the hallway. A door marked "Janitor's Closet." He went to the door and jiggled the handle, just for fun.

Inside the closet, the Ochre whimpered.

A sound like jostling marbles rattled behind the shroud. The Fra was laughing through his broken jaw. At last, no more delays. The Fra flung the door open. He raised the knife.

Vickie turned on the light.

Mark Fogarty's flashlight. Vickie thumbed the powerful LED maglite and aimed it directly at the Damned Fra's eye, an eye adapted to hours of dim light and shadows. The Fra recoiled, his world of darkness erupting in hateful white light.

Lord, keep it away!

There was no answer. And no protection. This was not pain that could be overcome through Faith. It was simply blindness.

The same blindness that cost you your hand...

NO! He had faith! The Fra slashed the air. The Carcass God would deliver the paint, he was sure of it.

The blade swept through the empty air without resistance, making a keening whistle that matched the wail from the Fra's mouth.

Then, a blessing! Something unyielding and angular struck him hard in the throat. The Fra was still blind, but the attack gave him a direction to reach towards. The Fra lashed out with his free hand and was rewarded with a panicked gurgle and the feel of pliant flesh, slick with blood, beneath his grip. He seized on that flesh and pushed forward, driving relentlessly until he felt the Ochre slam against the resolute force of a wall.

Yes!

The Damned Fra held the White Ochre there at the edge of his grasp, basking in exultation. She swung futilely against the arm pinning her in place, but her attacks meant nothing against The Fra's will and the Might of the Carcass God. The exploding flashes of light still blinded his vision, but they were already beginning to fade. The Fra waited patiently for his sight to return, the grip on his knife growing tighter by the second. His mistake before had been putting the Decayed God to the test like that. A few moment's delay was not an issue. He waited for his vision to clear.

Then one more thrust. One more use of the blade, and the Mural can begin.

It was the tingling just under his jaw that the Fra first found amiss.

It was not pain… not really. It was more of a spreading numbness working both ways, up to his head and also down towards his fingertips. He began to lose the feeling of the knife and the Ochre in his hands. The Fra squeezed both tighter, refusing to let his weakness allow either to escape his grasp.

The blinding colors finally began to fade from his vision. He could see his own arm, muscular and powerful as ever, except he could no longer feel his fingers.

He saw the Ochre, still pinned helplessly in his grasp. At her feet, he saw a long handle topped with a square, blunt blade. The ice breaking tool must have been the weapon she'd struck him with. As if an ordained artist of the God of Decay could be struck down by a mere ice breaker.

The Fra soaked in the details of her features, meaning to draw inspiration from it later. The sweat-soaked hair plastered to her forehead. The desperate flare of her nostrils. And her eyes. He longed for the fear there. The Damned Fra Anjelico looked deep into the White Ochre's eyes, searching for the terror that he would nurture in his own heart as he, at long last, set to work on the Mural.

...It was wrong. All wrong. The Fra saw fear, yes. But the fear was not pure. It was tainted. Something else lingered in the Ochre's gaze. Something like...

Anticipation?

The hazy pressure in the Fra's head tightened up. Consciously, he tried to draw a breath and realized he couldn't. The inside of his throat felt like a vacuum. Careful to keep the Ochre in his clutches, the Fra felt his neck with the back of his knife hand.

The curved half circle of his throat had crumpled up like a crushed soda can. The Fra felt no pain, but he tried desperately to suck in air to no avail. He couldn't breathe. His airway was completely closed off. He hadn't drawn a breath since... how long had he waited for his vision to clear?

Black spots began to crowd the edges of his sight.

No. Nononono NO!

The knife still lurked in his white-knuckled grip, waiting to be let loose. The knife ached to fly out and slice her open from hip to hip. For a moment, he nearly indulged that urge. But he was only minutes away from suffocating like a fish left in the desert. So close and he wasn't going to live long enough to paint so much as a single brush stroke. Even if he gutted her, it wouldn't matter. He'd failed the Carcass God. The Eternal Casket would be forever closed to him.

Then make her suffer! Make her pay! She laughs in the face of the Decayed God. Cut out her eyes! Rip open her insides! Take her fingers and...

Her fingers.

Fall! Vickie pleaded. *Die! Please just lay down and die!* She hung there, two feet off the ground, kicking desperately at the air, waiting for-

The killer let her go. The hand around her throat unclenched and Vickie was pumping her legs even before she hit the ground.

He grabbed her before she could run away. He hauled her back.

"No!" Vickie screamed. She tried to struggle free, but the maniac's strength was resolute as ever. He grabbed Vickie's wrists and held them in front of his face.

The Damned Fra Anjelico understood. Even though darkness crowded his oxygen-starved brain, the dirt was finally shoveled away from his vision and the Fra understood what the Carcass God had sent him to do.

The Fra had not failed. The Rotting Hand had moved him exactly where he needed to be.

...Amen.

Vickie tried to recoil, but the killer held her firm. His sticky, clammy hands roved over her palms and fingers, leaving a residue in their wake like the mucus trail of a slug.

Such exquisite fingers, the Fra marveled. Nimble, supple, clever hands. And her eyes. She watched him caressing her fingers. The Fra was certain that she saw and categorized everything to memory. There was not a single detail that the Ochre wouldn't be able to recall.

No. She's not the Ochre.

"Rrr," he croaked. "Rrrrr."

Reviled. Reviled Claricia.

It was no use. The suffocation that had narrowed his vision to a small pinhole of light had also robbed him of his ability to speak. He could not name her. He could not bid her back to the studio. He could not tell her what the Mural was supposed to be,

The Damned Fra Anjelico released her hands. He stumbled sideways and slumped against the wall of the cramped closet.

It would be okay. The Fra didn't need to tell her anything. A small spasm raced through his body. He sank further down.

His vision faded further. It was almost gone now. He could barely make out the Reviled Claricia as she watched him sink.

The Damned Fra Anjelico wished her nothing but success.

<u>24</u>

Vickie ran towards the art room like a scrambling teacher late for her first day of class. She'd risked a detour to the nurse's office for gauze and bandages, but she compensated by pushing herself to run through the dark hallways of Saint Regina at an even greater speed.

Her bleeding throat ached with every breath. Her muscles burned. Mental and physical stress had left her an utter shell of a person. Her body wanted nothing more than to curl up and go to sleep in the darkest corner that she could find.

None of it mattered. Vickie ran as fast as she could, an unraveling roll of bandages trailing behind her like a ghost.

Please. She prayed the whole time.

Please. Please. Please.

She finally reached the art classroom. Both hands full, Vickie forced the door open with her elbow and exploded into the classroom, spilling first aid supplies across the nearest table.

"Bridget!" she screamed.

Bridget wasn't on the table where the Fra had left her. Still, it was not a large classroom. Vickie could take in the entirety of the room without even having to turn her head.

She did anyway. She thoroughly scanned the room from one end to the other.

Because what if she was mistaken? What if there was something she overlooked? What if she hadn't searched carefully enough? Wouldn't she feel silly then? Better, far better, to meticulously examine every bloody, defiled inch of the classroom. Just to be absolutely certain.

In the end, no matter how hard she looked, a certainty was exactly what it was. Bridget was exactly where Vickie first saw her-

Down on the floor. In the corner. Nestled into Chris' chest with his arm slung protectively over her body.

There was no need to get closer. Vickie realized immediately that Bridget was dead. She was too intimately familiar with Bridget's lifeforce to think otherwise. There was no chance of pretending that Bridge's laughter, or even her pain, could somehow be hiding within that motionless figure lying on the floor. The lifelessness was just too stark- too much of an anathema to the exuberance and energy that defined who Bridget was.

But what was she supposed to do about it? Scream? Cry? Lie to herself? None of it felt right. None of it felt like enough. What did you say? What were you supposed to do when your best friend died while your back was turned? No last words. No goodbye. No Twelfth Bridget to replace her, no previous save to reload, no crossroads to cut a deal.

Just…. Nothing.

Chris was dead too. His skin grey and dull in the light of the dying fire. A thin trickle of blood ran from the corner of his mouth. His dead eyes were not set out into the distance. Rather, they were tilted downwards and to the side. He'd spent his final moments staring down at the top of Bridget's head.

Vickie sank to her knees. The dull thud was the only sound in the whole school.

It's just me. I'm the only living thing left in Saint Regina's Catholic Academy.

She laughed. With no one else to join in, she laughed longer and louder.

"Class of 2019!" she shrieked to herself. "Most likely to succeed! Best Kisser! Best friend!"

Vickie laughed until she was shrieking. And then she shrieked until the windows rattled in their panes. She rose up, no longer laughing, and stormed over to her best friend's corpse. She took the dead log of Chris' arm and pried it off her shoulder. She gripped Bridget by the collar and dragged her body away from Chris' side. Her best friend lay on the floor, arms splayed in a crooked "Y." Her eyes rolled back in her head and her mouth hung slightly ajar.

Horrible as it was, it was still better than seeing her in his arms.

"He got you killed!" Vickie screamed. "We could have been anyplace else in the world! Your house! My house! But we had to be here because you were stupid enough to think you loved this asshole!"

She spat in Chris' face.

She rounded on the other corner of the room. Where Todd lay, bald and stripped. His torso broken open. His insides poured out.

"And you!" Vickie raged. "*Why!?* Why couldn't you have taken a train like a normal person? Shitters!" she screamed at them. "*Stupid! Fucking! Shitheads!*"

Vickie staggered back until she hit against the windows. Her whole body convulsed. She heaved out some wretched sound- the bastard child of a scream and a sob. Her spine pressed against the cold glass, but it barely touched the raging furnace inside her. The heat refused to be quelled. There was just too much of it. These were her best friends. Fucking *butchered.* For what?

For the Mural.

Vickie jumped up. Her head whipped furiously around the room.

"Who said that?"

Nobody answered her. There was nobody in the room with her. There were no figures standing on the snow swept fields outside the window.

But somebody had spoken to her.

"No," she mumbled. It comforted her some. Her voice, broken and ruined as it was, was real. The other voice was not. It couldn't be.

For the Art.

Vickie clamped her hands over her ears, but it was pointless. The voice wasn't in her ears. It wasn't even really a voice. It was a slow, creeping sensation of fingers counting the vertebrate in her back. It was a stench in her nostrils, like a basement freezer left unplugged for too long. She could describe it so vividly… because it was still with her. A voice that didn't speak in words, and yet could be heard all the same. The voice found the empty space left by Bridget's passing and filled it with rancid knowledge. It explained. It beckoned.

It called her to serve.

After all, there was still Alcazar Brown to be scavenged from the spilled pot. And what about the Lenox Tan? The Lenox Tan was completely untouched.

And she still had plenty of red.

In an instant, Vickie understood everything. The *why* behind all this death filled her, the knowledge of it curdled inside of Vickie. Her stomach clenched down. Vickie doubled over, dry heaving, as if the knowledge could be physically repelled from her system.

No, no, no, the fingers crawling over her neck soothed. The rotting stench assured Vickie that its intentions were pure. It only wanted to bring meaning to the death all around Vickie. *Take up the brushes,* it bid. Take up the colors. The stone wall to her left cried out to her- an empty canvas, aching to be painted on in blood and liquid flesh. A monument to decay and despair, literally crafted from lives cut short. A message so powerful that television and the internet would compulsively spread it across entire civilizations.

Most who saw it would be shocked. Horrified. They would condemn the art loudly for all to hear.

...But, pulsing deep below the shouts and denunciations, some people would feel it. Some would feel the same thing that others might feel looking up at the roof of the Sistine Chapel.

The feeling that a God was real.

I could do it. That time, it was Vickie's own voice speaking in her head. *This place wouldn't be Saint Regina's anymore. It would belong to... something else.*

The Carcass God.

Vickie had the ability. And she had the hate. This was not her place. And these were not her people.

All she had to do now was pick up a brush. And there was already one between her feet. A tufty brush of brown hair with a handle the color of...

Butterscotch Cream.

Yes, that's exactly what it was. Vickie knelt down and picked up the brush. The cold air had done its work. The dead flesh was as hard and rigid in her grasp as any brush handle she'd ever known.

And wouldn't it feel good to paint? Good, oh so good, to permanently disfigure this place?

It would.

Vickie went over to the pots. The vat of red was full to brimming. Vickie shook it experimentally, pleased with the smooth motion of the paint. The death stench filled her. It hung like a haze over her thoughts, clouding everything except the urge to create. The scent may have been different, but it was a feeling Vickie knew well. She dipped her brush into the red and crossed to the wall in quick, purposeful steps.

There was no hesitation now. No questions. Vickie raised the brush and marked the wall with purposeful, swift strokes of red. The rotting odor intensified with every stroke. The Carcass God was pleased. Vickie felt it in the cold, tingling touch running up her spine.

It was not Vickie's pleasure. She looked at what she'd done, only the beginning strokes, and knew instinctively that it was wrong. She stepped back from her work, only three lines, and evaluated those three lines more critically than anyone else would have examined a finished portrait.

It wasn't right. Better to start over now.

Then begin again. The crawling sensation in her flesh was not discouraged. It assured Vickie that she had been chosen for a reason. The mural was inside her. Vickie just had to find it.

She needed no voice to promise her that. Vickie felt it just fine all by herself. Her own talent told her so.

There was a masterpiece to be made here. And she would be the one to create it.

<u>25</u>

"POLICE! Anyone on the premises, lay down and put your hands over your heads!"

Sergeant Jason Rodie pushed into the school at the head of a column of five officers, all with guns and flashlights drawn. Despite his authoritative entrance, Rodie dreaded what they were going to find. Four paramedics lingered just outside the door, waiting for the all clear to enter.

Forty-five minutes. It had taken them forty-five minutes to mobilize a response team and make the grueling trek through the blizzard to Saint Regina. Twice, their convoy had been delayed because one of their vehicles had gotten mired in a snow drift.

Forty-five minutes trapped with a killer.

They swept the cafeteria, flashlight beams skittering through the darkness like cockroaches.

"Oh, Jesus. We've got a body here!" Watson shouted.

"I need a paramedic!" Rodie ordered. Even as he said it, he knew it was an exercise in futility. The white male had a broken mop handle rammed through his throat. He was already a goner. But protocol was protocol.

"Watson, stay with the body," he said. "Rivera and Ornoff, I want you to sweep the west side of the floor. Coleman! With me!"

The paramedics knew to split up behind the two teams. Coleman stayed directly to his right as they pushed through the double doors and cautiously made their way down the dark hallway.

They rounded the corner and found the second body sprawled inside the janitor's closet. "Jesus," Rodie breathed as they approached the body.

It was another DOA. Rodie saw the filthy, fluid-soaked hood, and his first thought was that this had been some kind of execution. But then he took in the sheer size of the vic. And the knife lying between his feet. He considered how much of the blood on the dead man's shrouded face was already dried.

He keyed the radio on his shoulder. "I think our perp is down," he said. "But stay alert until we've swept the building.

His radio crackled. *"I've got blood here. It's leading up to the second floor."*

"We'll meet you there," Rodie radioed back. "Stay smart."

A paramedic had her hand under the hood, checking the prone figure for a pulse. She looked to Rodie and shook her head.

"Let's find a staircase," he said to Coleman.

They traversed the remainder of the hallway without incident. At the top of the stairs, Rodie radioed in again.

"Rivera, we're on the second floor. What's your status?"

Rivera squawked back. But, for a long time, all they heard over the comm channel was hissing static from the other side. River had his radio line open, but he wasn't speaking back.

Or maybe he can't....

The static droned on as Rodie and Coleman exchanged an ominous look.

Finally, River's voice came in over the airwaves.

"....Southeast corner," he said.

Rodie and the others converged on the scene to find Rivera, Ornoff, and the paramedics in a cluster just outside one of the classrooms. Coleman was a rookie, that's why Rodie had kept him close. Rivera and Ornoff had 30 years of experience between them. Rodie trusted them to handle anything they were confronted with.

The glassy stares on Ornoff's and Rivera's faces made it abundantly clear. Whatever waited for them in the classroom, they were not handling it. The paramedics couldn't face it either. One of them stood with his jaw hanging somewhere near his belt. The other had his hands clasped together and muttered a steady stream of low prayers under his breath.

Rodie pushed himself forward. He tried to project assuredness, both to the others and himself. As he shouldered his way clear of the doorway, he found himself wishing, for the first time in his career, that he could turn around and put someone else in charge. The air here was wrong. Charged. It felt like there was a train coming down the tracks and none of them could move out of the way. Rodie sucked in a shaky breath and braced himself for what he was about to see. He entered the classroom. Surveyed the scene.

"...Oh my fucking God."

He wasn't ready.

There was no being ready.

There were bodies everywhere. Chopped up parts everywhere. Pools of blood littered the floor, along with puddles of gelatinous fluid that Rodie didn't want to examine too closely. Medieval looking iron pots stood in line along the wall and glowing embers bathed the room in a primitive yellow glow.

Kneeling down at the opposite wall, as if encapsulated in her own private world, there was a girl. She was alive, but that was almost worse. She carried on with her business, humming to herself without a care in the world, even though blood ran freely from a wound in her throat. Her whole chest was slick with it.

And what she'd done to the wall....

<u>26</u>

"La la," Vickie sang tonelessly under her breath. "La, la, la." She added a few more brush strokes of shading. And then a splash of tan… Perfect. Vickie sat back, wiping her forehead and absentmindedly smearing some color over her eyebrow.

It was done. And impressively quick.

In seventh grade there'd been an assembly. Afternoon classes were canceled, and the entire student body had gathered for a presentation on how to be good little Children of God in a Bad Sinful World. The presenter had all the usual propaganda messages- don't do drugs, don't have sex, don't take the Lord's name in vain, but the way he jazzed it up was with paintings; murals that he conjured up to illustrate his points as he spoke. He worked on massive canvases that he transformed into crucifixes and lost lambs in rapid-fire, fifteen minute flurries of color and brushstrokes.

That was not Vickie's normal method. Typically, she worked like a turtle. Especially in physical medium instead of digital. So much harder to correct a mistake without an "undo" button.

This piece had been different. The first approach had been all wrong. Once Vickie realized that, inspiration flowed through her and into the brush like a lightning bolt funneled through a copper wire. Every brush stroke had been perfect. Every choice of color was beyond reproach. It was far and away the best work she'd ever done.

"Ma'am?"

Vickie sat back on her haunches. She'd been aware of the police, but now she turned to face them for the first time.

"I'm afraid you're late," she said.

The police officer had the decency to lower his eyes. His gun, however, still hovered somewhere between pointing at the floor and not quite pointing at Vickie.

"Ma'am, I'd like to get a paramedic to take a look at you. Would that be alright?"

"In a minute," Vickie said, barely paying attention to him. She picked up the brush she'd just put down. You were never really done the first time you thought you were done.

Rodie watched her go back to painting. He glanced towards the door, confirming that Coleman had her covered, and then holstered his own gun and knelt down beside her. "Can you tell me what happened here?" he asked.

"An act of God," she said. "Just not the God you're thinking of. Or maybe it is. Who the hell really knows?"

"That's certainly food for thought," he said. Rodie kept his voice carefully cool and even. Not that the woman with the paintbrush seemed upset. "But if there's anyone else in the school that we need to be looking for, I need you to tell us."

Her face trembled for a moment then. Rodie saw all that he needed to see. "There's nobody else," she whispered. "I'm the only one left." With a trembling sigh, she set down the paintbrush.

The cop kept looking back to the Mural. His eyes would settle on Vickie, but inevitably they drifted back towards her work. "You saw him downstairs?" Vickie asked. "In the hood?"

"Yes, ma'am. We saw him."

Vickie gestured up to the mural. She'd taken advantage of the full length of the wall, spreading the paint out from corner to corner. "He was supposed to be the one to do this," she said. "We…" Vickie gestured at her friends strewn around the room. "We were supposed to *be* this. Look at it. Go on."

"I see it," he began cautiously. "But we can talk about it later. You're bleeding. We have to-"

"I said, *look at it,*" Vickie roared. She stood up in a flash. Behind her, the cops in the doorway involuntarily flinched and stopped just short of pulling a trigger.

"There's your masterpiece!" she screamed. "Magic me a phone and I'll post it online myself for you! I hope everyone sees it!"

Rodie watched her rage. The girl paced and screamed. She ran her hands through her hair, leaving long streaks of color in her black locks. "I hope it goes viral!" she shrieked. "That's what you want, isn't it?"

Who she was talking to, Rodie had no idea. It wasn't him. It wasn't any of them in the room with her. *She could be on drugs,* he realized. He holstered his gun. She was not the assailant, Rodie was convinced of that much. Still, he couldn't let her go on screaming like this. If it kept going much longer, Rodie was going to have to restrain her.

Almost as if she had read his mind, the screeching stopped. The girl collapsed to her knees, falling as abruptly as a truck driving over thin ice. The paints were below her, but she didn't seem to care. She simply dropped, sending plastic bottles of Crayola paint rolling across the floor.

Vickie buried her head in her hands, blocking out the horror of the art room and replacing it with the darkness of her palms.

It felt so much better in the dark. It was better not to see. Better not to even be. She was nothing but the pressure of her palms against her eyes and the sound of her own ragged breath rattling in her ears.

But, try as she might to deny it, there was still paint soaking through the leg of her jeans. And she felt a plastic paintbrush prodding painfully into her knee cap.

Vickie was still at Saint Regina Catholic Academy. And her work wasn't done yet.

She took her face out of her hands and turned to the cops."Just look at it, please," she begged them. "This is what happened in the end."

Vickie herself did not look. She didn't have to. She knew exactly what it was.

She had painted a mural. But she hadn't done it with the flesh and blood from the iron pots. And she hadn't touched the brushes made from the fingers of one of her oldest friends.

She had done her work with the paints and brushes left behind in the supply closet. She had used washable children's paint- blue and brown and green and yellow and every color except for red. She'd painted the sky and the sun. She'd painted a tree from the floor to as high as she could reach. She'd made a massive canopy of branches- bustling, spring green leaves dotted with a smattering of pink flowers. Starting at the top of the trunk and working her way down, Vickie had painted a column of initials in broad, bold strokes- PA, AF, EC, TR, CC, BF.

Peter Arrogate.

Alex Fogarty.

Ellen Cutter.

Todd Reed.

Chris Castellano.

...Bridget Fallon.

Vickie had finished her mural by adding two figures at the base of the tree. A man and a woman, intertwined in each other's arms. The female figure was a delicate thing of pale skin and red hair, wrapped protectively in the arms of the larger figure with his powerful arms and adoring gaze.

Vickie drew them mostly from memory, it was less painful that way, but there were times that a refresher was necessary to get a detail right. When that happened, Vickie would grit her teeth and looked back over her shoulder at Bridget and Chris' final embrace. Placing Bridget's body back in Chris' arms had been surprisingly easy. It was still horrifying, but it was no harder than closing Bridget's eyes. Or kissing her forehead one final time.

It was certainly easier than having to look back at their bodies.

But it was done now. It was all done.

"This is all that's left," she said. "There's nothing else for me to do here."

The cop took that for consent. He motioned for the paramedics to come in and take over. The rest of the police officers filed in along with them.

Vickie didn't resist as the paramedics poured over her. They wrapped the bloody gouge in her throat. They wrapped a blanket around her shoulders and helped her to her feet. Vickie was content to follow. They were taking her Away. Away was all that mattered.

Meanwhile, the main cop was shouting orders. He called for *"the chain of evidence"* and *"crime scene integrity."* But one of his officers wasn't listening. The cop had probably started the night young, only a few years older than Vickie herself, but he staggered towards her now like an ancient drunk reeling his way out of the bar. He grabbed Vickie by the arm.

"What is it?" the cop asked. Despite all the horrors around him, even now, all he could look at was the wall of color rising up above the butchery. "Just what the hell is it supposed to be?"

"That's the point of art, isn't it?" Vickie asked as the paramedics led her towards the door. "It's open to interpretation." The paramedics didn't slow down for the cop's questions. They continued to resolutely guide Vickie towards the comforts of the waiting ambulance. Still, she looked over her shoulder at his slack jaw and bewildered eyes. "I'll give you one hint though," she called out. "The name of this piece? It's called 'Growth,'" she said.

They were Vickie's last words before the paramedics brought her into the hallway. They were taking her away from Saint Regina's Catholic Academy, and Vickie let them take her away.

With every step, she waited for the smell of death in her nose to fade away. She waited for the icy tingle crawling over her skin to still.

Vickie feared that she had a long wait ahead of her.

About the Author

Sean McDonough lives on Long Island, NY with his wife and daughters. Follow him on Facebook at https://www.facebook.com/houseoftheboogeyman/ or on Instagram @houseoftheboogeyman.

Printed in the USA
CPSIA information can be obtained
at www.ICGtesting.com
JSHW020404110224
56982JS00004B/22